Technology and Future Trends: Reflections on the Future of Technology and Society

Ivette Smith

Paperback ISBN:**978-1-969775-80-2**

Table of Contents

Introduction iv

Chapter 1: Decoding the Tech Landscape 1

Chapter 2: Ethical Dimensions of Modern Tech 29

Chapter 3: Technology in Everyday Life 45

Chapter 4: Preparing for the Digital Future 64

Chapter 5: Addressing Tech-Driven Global Challenges 80

Chapter 6: The Future of Work and Society 99

Chapter 7: Forward-Thinking Insights 116

Conclusion 141

References 143

Introduction

In the blink of an eye, we've gone from marveling at the first computers to carrying the world's knowledge in our pockets. As Arthur C. Clarke once said, "Any sufficiently advanced technology is indistinguishable from magic." This magic, however, is a double-edged sword.

Consider the story of a small village in a remote part of the world. One day, they received solar-powered tablets preloaded with educational materials. For the first time, children who had never seen a book were learning to read, and adults were accessing information about better farming techniques and healthcare. The potential to improve lives was unmistakable. Yet, this same village, now connected to the global grid, quickly became susceptible to the darker sides of technology—cybersecurity threats, misinformation, and the loss of cultural heritage.

This book examines the fascinating and often paradoxical world of technology. It explores the immense potential innovations have to improve our lives, while also addressing the concurrent challenges and ethical dilemmas they pose to society. I aim to provide a comprehensive overview of emerging technologies, offering insights into what the future may hold and preparing you for the changes to come. Through a blend of historical context, current developments, and future projections, we will navigate the intricate landscape of technological advancement, celebrating its triumphs and critically examining its pitfalls.

In just a few decades, the pace of technological advancement has accelerated at an unprecedented rate. From the advent of personal computers in the 1980s to the explosion of the internet in the 1990s, and now to the era of artificial intelligence, quantum computing, and biotechnology, each leap forward has reshaped the way we live, work, and interact with the world. Consider how smartphones, which were rare luxuries a little over a decade ago, are now ubiquitous, serving as personal assistants, communication hubs, and entertainment centers. Similarly, the rise of social media platforms has revolutionized global communication, influencing everything from personal relationships to political movements.

The rapid development of technologies such as 5G, the Internet of Things (IoT), and blockchain is creating a hyper-connected world where devices and systems communicate seamlessly. Innovations in healthcare, such as CRISPR gene editing and telemedicine, are pushing the boundaries of what is medically possible, promising to cure diseases and extend human life. Meanwhile, advancements in renewable energy technologies are paving the way for a more sustainable future. This relentless pace shows no signs of slowing down, making it crucial to stay informed and adaptable.

Understanding future trends in technology is key for several reasons. First, it enables individuals and organizations to anticipate and prepare for changes that can disrupt industries and economies. By staying ahead of the curve, businesses can innovate and remain competitive, while individuals can develop the skills needed for emerging job markets.

Secondly, an awareness of technological trends allows society to address potential ethical and social implications proactively. As technologies like AI and biotechnology become more integrated into daily life, questions around privacy, security, and moral responsibility become increasingly urgent. By engaging with these issues early, policymakers, educators, and the public can help shape the development and implementation of technology in ways that benefit society as a whole.

Lastly, understanding future trends empowers you to make informed decisions about your personal and professional lives. From choosing a career path to investing in new technologies, having a grasp of where technology is headed can guide more strategic and beneficial choices. In a world where technology is a driving force behind economic, social, and cultural change, staying informed is not just an advantage—it's a necessity. Join me on this journey to understand the profound impact of technology on our past, present, and future.

Chapter 1:
Decoding the Tech Landscape

As we stand on the edge of a new era, the rapid evolution of technology continues to shape our reality in ways previously confined to the realms of science fiction. The digital tapestry of our lives is interwoven with threads of innovation that significantly alter our daily interactions, societal structures, and even our human potential. This chapter explores the dynamic and transformative world of technology, focusing on the development and integration of artificial intelligence (AI) into our lives, which serves as both a catalyst for unprecedented change and a mirror reflecting our complex relationship with progress.

1.1 The Evolution of Artificial Intelligence: From Theory to Daily Impact

Historical Overview

The genesis of artificial intelligence can be traced back to the aspirations and theoretical frameworks proposed by pioneers who dared to envision machines capable of thinking. In the mid-20th century, Alan Turing, a British mathematician and logician, proposed what is now known as the Turing Test—a criterion of intelligence that assesses a machine's ability to exhibit human-like intelligence. The implications of this test were profound, pushing scientists to think critically about the criteria that define thought and consciousness. Following this, the development of neural networks laid the foundational stones for what would become the complex algorithms driving today's AI innovations. These early models, simplistic yet revolutionary, evolved through decades of research and development, leading to the sophisticated systems we see today.

Current Implementations

Today, artificial intelligence has transcended the boundaries of research labs and become a staple presence in everyday life. AI's integration into consumer technology, such as smartphones and home assistants, has made it an almost invisible yet indispensable part of daily routines. For instance, AI-driven predictive text and voice recognition technologies have streamlined communication, making it faster and more efficient. In customer service, AI chatbots that interpret and respond to human queries have transformed the landscape of consumer interaction, offering 24/7 service solutions that were previously unimaginable.

Impact Analysis

The impact of AI extends beyond mere convenience; it has catalyzed transformative changes across various industries. In healthcare, AI's application in diagnostic imaging, AI algorithms can analyze medical images, such as X-rays, MRIs, and CT scans, with exceptional precision. These algorithms can detect abnormalities, such as tumors or fractures, at early stages, often before they are noticeable to human eyes. This early detection is crucial for diseases like cancer, where timely intervention can significantly improve patient outcomes. AI is being used to predict patient outcomes, personalize treatment plans, and even assist in surgery. Machine learning models can analyze vast amounts of patient data to identify patterns and suggest the most effective treatments. For instance, AI can help oncologists determine the best chemotherapy regimen based on the genetic makeup of a patient's cancer. In surgery, robots equipped with AI can assist surgeons by providing enhanced precision, reducing the risk of human error, and improving recovery times.

The automotive industry has seen a paradigm shift with the integration of AI in the development of autonomous vehicles. These self-driving cars rely on AI to interpret data from sensors, cameras, and radar to navigate roads safely. AI algorithms process this data in real-time, making decisions about speed, direction, and obstacle avoidance. The benefits of autonomous vehicles extend beyond convenience to include significant improvements in safety and efficiency. By reducing human error, which is a leading cause of accidents, autonomous vehicles have the potential to save lives and reduce injuries. Additionally, AI can optimize traffic flow, reduce congestion, and improve fuel efficiency by predicting and responding to traffic patterns.

AI is also transforming the logistics and transportation sectors. Autonomous trucks and drones are being developed for the delivery of goods, promising to reduce costs and increase efficiency. Companies like Tesla and Waymo are at the forefront of this revolution, continuously advancing the capabilities of autonomous driving technologies. Similarly, in finance, AI-driven algorithms now perform complex stock market analyses at speeds and accuracies far surpassing human capabilities, optimizing investment strategies and managing financial risks with unprecedented precision. Machine learning models can analyze historical data to predict potential risks and fraud, allowing financial institutions to take proactive measures. For example, AI can detect unusual transaction patterns that may indicate fraudulent activity, enabling banks to prevent financial crimes. AI-powered chatbots and virtual assistants are improving customer service in the finance industry. These tools can handle a wide range of inquiries, from account information to investment advice, providing customers with quick and accurate responses. This enhances customer satisfaction and allows human employees to focus on more complex tasks.

The retail industry is another sector experiencing significant transformation due to AI. Personalized shopping experiences are becoming the norm, with AI analyzing customer data to provide tailored recommendations. E-commerce giants like Amazon use AI to suggest products based on browsing history, purchase behavior, and even sentiment analysis from customer reviews.

AI is also improving inventory management and supply chain operations. Predictive analytics help retailers forecast demand, reducing overstock and stockouts. This ensures that customers can find the products they need while minimizing excess inventory costs for retailers.

In physical stores, AI-powered systems like cashier-less checkouts and smart shelves are enhancing the shopping experience. For example, Amazon Go stores use AI and computer vision to allow customers to simply walk out with their purchases, with the payment automatically processed through their Amazon accounts.

In education, AI is playing a pivotal role in the education sector by providing personalized learning experiences. Adaptive learning platforms use AI to assess a student's strengths and weaknesses, tailoring educational content to their individual needs. This helps students learn at their own pace and receive targeted support in areas where they struggle.

Additionally, AI is being used to automate administrative tasks, such as grading and scheduling, freeing up educators to focus on teaching and mentoring. AI-driven analytics can also provide insights into student performance, helping educators identify at-risk students and intervene early to improve outcomes.

Future Projections

Looking ahead, the trajectory of AI development suggests both extraordinary potential and formidable challenges. The advent of autonomous decision-making systems and further advancements in machine learning will likely introduce new layers of functionality that could automate entire industries. However, these advancements will also necessitate rigorous ethical considerations. Issues such as privacy, security, and the moral implications of AI decision-making will require robust dialogue and thoughtful regulation. As AI systems become more capable of performing tasks traditionally requiring human empathy and ethical judgment, the delineation of roles between humans and machines will become increasingly blurred, prompting critical questions about the future of work and the ethical boundaries of machine autonomy.

As we explore these evolving landscapes, the promise and perils of artificial intelligence will undoubtedly play a pivotal role in shaping the future. The balance we strike between leveraging AI's capabilities and safeguarding our ethical values will determine the trajectory of our societal evolution. This exploration is not merely academic, but a necessary discourse as we forge paths into a future where technology and humanity increasingly intersect.

1.2 Blockchain Beyond Bitcoin: Securing a Digital Future

Blockchain Fundamentals

Blockchain technology, often synonymous with cryptocurrencies like Bitcoin, actually offers a far broader range of applications due to its unique structure and functionality. At its core, blockchain is a decentralized digital ledger that records transactions across multiple computers in such a way that the registered transactions cannot be altered retroactively. This architecture promotes transparency and enhances security, as there is no central point of failure. Each block in the chain contains many transactions, and every time a new transaction occurs on the blockchain, a record of that transaction is added to every participant's ledger. This decentralized consensus mechanism ensures that the information recorded on the blockchain is highly resistant to tampering and fraud. With a little more detail, here are the steps for creating a Blockchain:

1. **Transaction Initiation:** A transaction is initiated when someone wants to transfer an asset or data to someone else.

For example, sending cryptocurrency, updating a record, or executing a smart contract.

2. **Transaction Verification:** The transaction is broadcasted to a network of computers (nodes). These nodes check the transaction's validity using algorithms and consensus mechanisms, such as Proof of Work or Proof of Stake.

3. **Block Creation:** Verified transactions are grouped into a block. Each block contains a list of these transactions and a unique code called a "hash."

4. **Linking Blocks:** Each block also contains the hash of the previous block, creating a chain of blocks. This linkage ensures that once a block is added, it cannot be altered without changing all subsequent blocks, which is practically impossible.

5. **Adding to the Blockchain:** Once the block is created, it is added to the existing blockchain and becomes a permanent part of the ledger. This is done by the nodes reaching a consensus on the validity of the block.

6. **Completion:** The transaction is complete, and the blockchain is updated across all nodes in the network. This ensures that all copies of the blockchain are identical and up to date.

Blockchain technology offers a robust framework for enhancing transparency, security, and efficiency across various industries. Its applications extend far beyond cryptocurrencies, providing innovative solutions for supply chain management, healthcare, voting, intellectual property, real estate, identity verification, finance, energy management, smart contracts, and government services. As blockchain technology continues to evolve, its potential to drive cathartic changes in how we conduct business and manage data becomes increasingly evident.

Applications Beyond Cryptocurrency

While blockchain technology began with Bitcoin, its potential applications permeate various sectors. In supply chain management, blockchain provides unparalleled transparency by allowing every participant in the chain to trace the product's journey from origin to consumer. This capability is particularly crucial in industries like pharmaceuticals and food production, where provenance and authenticity are essential. For example, a blockchain system can help track the production, processing, packaging, and distribution of a drug, ensuring that counterfeit medications do not enter the supply chain. Here are more detailed examples:

1. Supply Chain Management:

- Blockchain can enhance transparency and traceability in supply chains. By recording each step of a product's journey on a blockchain, companies can track goods from production to delivery. This helps in verifying the authenticity of products, detecting counterfeits, and ensuring ethical sourcing.

- *Example:* IBM's Food Trust blockchain is used by major retailers like Walmart to track the origin and journey of food products, improving food safety and reducing waste.

2. Healthcare:

- Blockchain can secure patient records, ensuring data integrity and privacy. It allows for the secure sharing of medical records among healthcare providers, improving patient care and reducing administrative costs.

- *Example:* Medicalchain and Patientory are using blockchain to create secure, patient-centered health record systems that give patients control over their data.

3. Voting Systems:

- Blockchain can provide secure and transparent voting platforms, reducing the risk of fraud and ensuring the integrity of election results. Voters can cast their votes online, and the blockchain ensures that each vote is counted accurately.

- *Example:* Voatz has piloted blockchain-based voting in several U.S. states, offering secure and accessible voting for military personnel and other remote voters.

4. Intellectual Property and Copyright Management:

- Blockchain can record and manage intellectual property rights, providing a transparent and immutable ledger of ownership and usage rights. This helps in protecting creators' rights and ensuring fair compensation.

- *Example:* Ascribe and Po.et are blockchain platforms designed to help creators register and manage their digital works, ensuring they get credit and compensation for their creations.

5. Real Estate:

- Blockchain can streamline property transactions by recording deeds and ownership transfers on a secure and transparent ledger. This reduces the need for intermediaries and simplifies the buying and selling process.

- *Example:* Propy and Ubitquity are using blockchain to facilitate property transactions and record-keeping, aiming to reduce fraud and increase efficiency in real estate markets.

6. Identity Verification:

- Blockchain can provide secure digital identities, enabling individuals to control access to their personal information.

This is particularly useful in areas such as banking, travel, and online services.

- *Example:* Sovrin and Civic are creating decentralized identity platforms that allow users to manage their digital identities securely and grant access to third parties as needed.

7. Finance and Banking:

- Beyond cryptocurrencies, blockchain can improve various financial services, such as cross-border payments, trade finance, and compliance. Blockchain reduces transaction times and costs and enhances security.

- *Example:* Ripple uses blockchain technology to facilitate real-time, cross-border payments for financial institutions, offering faster and cheaper alternatives to traditional banking systems.

8. Energy Management:

- Blockchain can enable peer-to-peer energy trading and efficient management of energy grids. By recording energy production and consumption on a blockchain, it ensures transparency and facilitates decentralized energy markets.

- *Example:* Power Ledger is a blockchain-based platform that allows users to trade surplus energy from renewable sources, promoting sustainable energy usage.

9. Smart Contracts:

- Smart contracts are self-executing contracts with the terms directly written into code. They automatically execute and enforce agreements when predefined conditions are met, reducing the need for intermediaries.

- *Example:* Ethereum is a leading blockchain platform that supports smart contracts, enabling developers to create decentralized applications (dApps) that run on its blockchain.

10. Government and Public Services:

- Blockchain can enhance transparency and efficiency in government operations, such as land registries, public records, and social welfare distribution. It reduces bureaucratic inefficiencies and corruption risks.

- *Example:* Estonia uses blockchain technology to secure its digital identity system, e-residency program, and various public services, leading to increased trust and efficiency in government operations.

In addition, blockchain is making significant inroads in the realm of voting systems. Traditional voting systems are often fraught with challenges related to security, voter privacy, and integrity of the results. Blockchain can mitigate these issues by providing a secure platform where votes can be cast as transactions, which once recorded, are immutable and transparently verifiable by all parties. However, the implementation of blockchain in voting systems isn't without challenges. Issues such as scalability—how to manage large volumes of transactions quickly—and user education on blockchain technology are significant hurdles. Additionally, regulatory acceptance varies by region, impacting how swiftly blockchain-based voting systems can be adopted.

Challenges and Solutions

Despite its potential, blockchain technology faces several challenges that could impede its broader adoption. Scalability remains a primary concern, as the current capability of blockchain systems to process transactions is limited compared to traditional databases. The proof of work system, which is used by Bitcoin and other cryptocurrencies, requires substantial computational power and energy, raising concerns about its environmental impact.

Emerging solutions aimed at addressing these challenges include the development of new consensus algorithms such as proof of stake, which significantly reduces the amount of computational power and thus energy required to verify transactions. Additionally, layer-two solutions like the Lightning Network propose a system where not all transactions need to be directly recorded on the blockchain, thereby enhancing the system's capacity to handle larger transaction volumes more swiftly.

Impact on Data Integrity

The integrity of data is paramount in today's digital age, where information is both currency and commodity. Blockchain technology's inherent characteristics—immutability, transparency, and security—make it an ideal solution for enhancing data integrity across various sectors. In the financial sector, for instance, blockchain provides a robust framework for fraud prevention and secure financial transactions. Banks and financial institutions are experimenting with blockchain to manage everything from international payments to daily operational transactions, reducing opportunities for fraud and errors in bookkeeping.

Real-world examples of blockchain implementation show promising results. For instance, Maersk, one of the world's largest shipping companies, partnered with IBM to implement a blockchain-based supply chain system that tracks shipping containers across the world in real-time. This system improves operational efficiency and enhances the security and transparency of shipping transactions, allowing customers and regulators to track the provenance of goods as they move globally. Such applications underscore blockchain's potential to revolutionize how we maintain and verify the integrity of data across diverse industry sectors, potentially leading to a future where digital transactions and records are both transparent and trustless.

1.3 Exploring the Potential of Quantum Computing

Principles of Quantum Mechanics

Quantum mechanics, a fundamental theory in physics, provides the basis for understanding the behavior of particles at the smallest scales of energy levels of atoms and subatomic particles. This understanding is crucial for the development of quantum computing. Unlike classical physics, which describes the macroscopic world, quantum mechanics reveals a landscape where particles may exist in multiple states simultaneously, a phenomenon known as superposition. Another fundamental aspect is entanglement, where particles become interconnected and the state of one (no matter how far apart they are) can instantaneously affect the state of another. These principles are not just theoretical curiosities; they are the very attributes that quantum computers leverage to perform operations at speeds unattainable by classical computers.

To make this concept accessible, consider a traditional light switch, which can be either in an 'on' or 'off' position. In contrast, a quantum bit, or qubit, the basic unit of quantum information, can exist simultaneously in both states until measured, thanks to superposition. This ability allows quantum computers to process a vast number of possibilities simultaneously. Entanglement further enhances this capability, enabling qubits that are entangled to communicate instantaneously across distances, thereby dramatically increasing the processing power.

Comparison with Classical Computing

Classical computers, which encompass everything from early calculators to modern supercomputers, encode information in binary 'bits', each represented by either a 0 or a 1. These bits are the DNA of classical computing, dictating every operation through a binary framework that, while powerful, has its limitations, particularly in solving problems that require the simultaneous processing of numerous variables.

Quantum computers, by contrast, use qubits, which can represent numerous possible combinations of 1 and 0 at once. This ability to hold and process multiple permutations concurrently allows quantum computers to solve complex problems much more efficiently than classical computers. For example, in drug discovery, a quantum computer can analyze and simulate the molecular structure of a new drug in ways that would take a classical computer much longer, if it's even possible at all.

Potential Applications

The potential applications of quantum computing are vast and have the power to change things dramatically across various sectors. In cryptography, quantum computing poses both an opportunity and a challenge. Quantum computers could theoretically break many of the cryptographic systems currently in use almost instantaneously, thus rendering traditional methods of securing data obsolete. However, this challenge drives the development of quantum cryptography, which could potentially create unhackable encryption systems.

In drug discovery, quantum computers can model molecular interactions at an atomic level in ways that are impossible for classical computers, potentially reducing the time and cost of developing new drugs significantly. Moreover, quantum computing holds promise for complex system modeling such as climate forecasting, where its ability to quickly process vast arrays of data could provide more accurate predictions of extreme weather patterns.

Current State and Challenges

Despite its potential, quantum computing is still in its nascent stages. Current quantum computers have a limited number of qubits and are prone to errors due to quantum decoherence and noise interference. Quantum decoherence, for instance, occurs when qubits lose their quantum mechanical properties, typically because of the interaction with their environment in ways that are not yet fully understood, which limits the reliability of quantum computations. Here is a simple breakdown of quantum computing:

Here's a simple breakdown:

1. **Bits vs. Qubits:** Traditional computers use bits as the basic unit of information, which can be either 0 or 1. Quantum computers use quantum bits, or qubits, which can be both 0 and 1 at the same time, thanks to a property called "superposition."

2. **Superposition:** Imagine a spinning coin. While it's spinning, it's not just heads or tails; it's in a state where it could be either. Qubits can be in multiple states simultaneously, allowing quantum computers to explore many possibilities at once.

3. **Entanglement:** Qubits can be entangled, meaning the state of one qubit can depend on the state of another, no matter how far apart they are. This allows qubits to work together in ways that classical bits can't.

4. **Parallel Processing:** Because of superposition and entanglement, quantum computers can perform many calculations at the same time, potentially solving complex problems much faster than traditional computers.

5. **Quantum Speed-Up:** For certain types of problems, quantum computers could solve them exponentially faster than classical computers by processing all possible solutions simultaneously and finding the right one more quickly.

The commercial viability of quantum computing remains a topic of intense research and development. Companies like Google, IBM, and others are at the forefront, investing heavily in quantum computing technologies. Google's quantum computer, Sycamore, claimed "quantum supremacy" in 2019 when it performed a specific task in 200 seconds that it claimed would take the most powerful supercomputer 10,000 years to complete. However, the road to a fully functional, broadly applicable quantum computer is still fraught with technical challenges that need to be overcome, including improving qubit coherence times, developing error correction methods, and creating scalable quantum computing systems.

As we continue to advance our understanding and technology, the bounds of quantum computing will expand, potentially altering the computational landscape dramatically. The ongoing research into making these systems more stable and scalable paves the way for their eventual integration into everyday technology, a step that could revolutionize industries and redefine how we approach problem-solving at fundamental levels.

1.4 The Rise of Autonomous Vehicles: Ethics, Potential, and Public Perception

Technological Foundations

Autonomous vehicles (AVs), often depicted in the realms of futuristic science fiction, are now navigating the very fabric of our modern infrastructure. At the core of their operation lies a sophisticated array of sensors, AI algorithms, machine learning models, and LIDAR (Light Detection and Ranging) systems, which collectively orchestrate the symphony of self-driving technology. LIDAR functions as the eyes of the vehicle, emitting laser beams to measure distances and create a high-resolution, 3D map of the surrounding environment. This technology, when integrated with cameras and radar, feeds vast amounts of data to the vehicle's AI systems.

These AI algorithms are trained through machine learning to make sense of complex traffic scenarios, learning from vast datasets that include every conceivable road situation. Through continuous processing of sensory information, these vehicles can detect objects, interpret traffic signals, and make split-second decisions about navigation and speed. For example, consider an AV navigating a busy urban intersection; it simultaneously assesses the speed of oncoming vehicles, the movement of pedestrians, and the timing of traffic lights to make safe and efficient decisions in real-time. This level of situational awareness and decision-making capacity highlights the profound advancements in both hardware and software that drive the autonomous vehicle industry.

Safety and Efficiency

The potential benefits of autonomous vehicles pivot significantly on improvements in road safety and traffic efficiency. Human error is implicated in approximately 94% of traffic accidents, according to data from the National Highway Traffic Safety Administration. Autonomous vehicles, governed by algorithms and devoid of human susceptibilities such as distractions, fatigue, or impairment, herald a substantial decline in these incidents. By eliminating these variables, AVs have the potential to drastically reduce accidents and fatalities on our roads.

In addition, autonomous vehicles can optimize driving patterns and streamline traffic flow, significantly enhancing traffic efficiency. Through vehicle-to-vehicle (V2V) and vehicle-to-infrastructure (V2I) communications, AVs can transmit information regarding traffic conditions, road hazards, and traffic signals, allowing for a coordinated flow that reduces unnecessary stoppages and improves fuel efficiency. Imagine a scenario where all vehicles on a highway communicate to maintain optimal speed and spacing, effectively eliminating the concept of traffic jams and drastically reducing commuting times.

Ethical Considerations

However, the integration of autonomous vehicles into public roadways introduces complex ethical dilemmas that challenge existing frameworks of moral and legal responsibility. One of the most discussed scenarios is the "trolley problem," where an autonomous vehicle must choose between two detrimental outcomes, such as hitting a pedestrian or swerving and harming its passengers. Deciding how AVs should respond to such dilemmas involves programming ethics into machine behavior, and raising questions about the values and priorities that should guide AI decision-making processes.

Privacy concerns also emerge with the adoption of AVs, as they rely on collecting and processing vast amounts of data about their environments, which inevitably includes information about individuals. The potential for surveillance and data breaches poses significant privacy risks, requiring robust data protection measures and transparency in how data is used and shared.

Public Acceptance

The trajectory of autonomous vehicles towards widespread adoption is not solely contingent on technological advancement but equally on public perception and acceptance. Safety records play a crucial role in shaping public trust. Incidents involving AVs, even if statistically minor compared to human-driven vehicle accidents, receive heightened media attention, potentially skewing public perception about the safety of autonomous technology.

Regulatory developments also influence public acceptance, as government endorsements and comprehensive safety standards can enhance trust in the technology's reliability and safety. Moreover, the portrayal of autonomous vehicles in the media can sway public opinion significantly, underscoring the need for accurate and balanced reporting to foster an informed public discourse.

As autonomous vehicles continue to evolve, their integration into society presents a multifaceted challenge that encompasses technological innovation, ethical considerations, and societal adaptation. The balance between these elements will ultimately dictate the role of autonomous vehicles in reshaping transportation and, by extension, the broader socio-economic landscape.

1.5 Biotechnology in the Modern Age: CRISPR, Genome Editing, and Beyond

Overview of CRISPR

The landscape of genetic research underwent a seismic shift with the advent of CRISPR-Cas9, a genetic editing technology that has been likened to having molecular scissors. Here, CRISPR (Clustered Regularly Interspaced Short Palindromic Repeats) which is a natural defense mechanism found in bacteria, and Cas9 (an enzyme) work in tandem to find and modify DNA at precise locations. Imagine the vast, twisted landscape of a human genome as a complex map; CRISPR-Cas9 offers scientists the tools to pinpoint an exact genetic street and alter its direction or appearance. This technology emerged from the study of bacterial defense systems, which use CRISPR sequences to remember and destroy viral DNA sequences. In the lab, researchers can guide Cas9 to a specific genetic location to cut the DNA, allowing them to remove unwanted sequences or add new ones. This process not only revolutionizes how we can manipulate genetic material but also drastically speeds up genetic research that once took years, reducing it to weeks or even days.

How CRISPR Works

1. **Natural Function:** In bacteria, CRISPR functions as an immune system. When a bacterium is attacked by a virus, it stores a segment of the virus's DNA in its CRISPR sequence.

If the virus attacks again, the bacterium can recognize and cut the viral DNA using this stored sequence.

2. **Components:**

   - **Guide RNA (gRNA):** A short RNA sequence that matches the DNA sequence where the edit needs to occur. It guides the CRISPR system to the exact location in the DNA.

   - **Cas9 Protein:** An enzyme that acts as molecular scissors, cutting the DNA at the location specified by the guide RNA.

3. **Gene Editing Process:**

   - **Design:** Scientists design a guide RNA to target a specific DNA sequence in the genome.

   - **Introduction:** The guide RNA and Cas9 protein are introduced into cells.

   - **Cutting:** The Cas9 protein cuts the DNA at the targeted location.

   - **Repair:** The cell's natural repair mechanisms fix the break. Scientists can manipulate this repair process to add, delete, or replace specific genetic material.

Applications of CRISPR

1. **Genetic Research:** CRISPR allows scientists to study genes by creating organisms with specific genetic modifications. This helps in understanding gene functions and disease mechanisms.

2. **Medicine:**

   - **Gene Therapy:** CRISPR is being explored to correct the genetic defect causing Duchenne Muscular

Dystrophy in young dogs, an important step towards human therapies. This method has similarly been applied in experimental therapies for cystic fibrosis and sickle cell disease, diseases caused by small genetic mutations that CRISPR can potentially correct.

- **Cancer Treatment:** In cancer treatment, CRISPR is at the forefront of personalized medicine, particularly in the development of immunotherapy treatments. It can be used to modify immune cells to better target and destroy cancer cells.

3. **Agriculture:**

- **Crop Improvement:** CRISPR can be used to create crops with desirable traits, such as resistance to pests or improved nutritional content.

- **Disease Resistance:** It helps in developing plants that are resistant to diseases and environmental stresses.

4. **Bioengineering:**

- **Synthetic Biology:** CRISPR allows for the creation of organisms with new or altered traits, such as bacteria that produce useful compounds.

5. **Ecology:**

- **Gene Drives:** CRISPR can be used to spread genetic changes rapidly through populations, potentially controlling pests or invasive species.

Advantages of CRISPR

- **Precision:** CRISPR targets specific DNA sequences with high accuracy.

- **Efficiency:** It is relatively simple and inexpensive compared to other gene-editing techniques.

- **Versatility:** It can be used in a wide range of organisms, from bacteria to plants to animals.

Ethical and Social Implications

As with any groundbreaking technology, CRISPR brings with it a labyrinth of ethical, legal, and social questions. The power to edit genes inevitably raises concerns about the potential for misuse, such as the creation of so-called "designer babies," where embryos could be edited to enhance physical traits or intelligence, raising significant ethical and societal concerns about inequality and access. The international scientific community has called for a moratorium on heritable genome editing until ethical and safety concerns are addressed, underscoring the need for robust ethical guidelines and oversight.

The regulation of CRISPR technology also varies significantly by country, reflecting diverse ethical and cultural perspectives on genetic modification. This patchwork of regulatory frameworks impacts the development and potential applications of genome editing technologies globally. As public debates continue to evolve, it is crucial that they not only consider the scientific and medical aspects of genome editing but also the broader societal implications, including consent, privacy, and the potential for genetic discrimination.

Future of Biotechnology

Looking forward, the field of biotechnology is poised for continued innovation, particularly through advancements in synthetic biology and the development of more refined genome editing techniques. Synthetic biology, which combines biology and engineering principles, allows for the creation and redesign of biological parts, devices, and systems that do not exist in the natural world. This could lead to revolutionary applications in medicine, such as the creation of entirely synthetic organisms that produce pharmaceuticals or function as living therapeutics.

Personalized medicine, powered by genome editing, is likely to become more prevalent as these technologies mature. The ability to tailor treatments based on an individual's genetic makeup could dramatically increase the efficacy of treatments and minimize side effects. In the future, we might see a convergence of various technologies, such as AI and biotech, leading to unprecedented capabilities in predictive healthcare, where diseases could be anticipated and prevented before they manifest.

As we navigate this promising yet uncertain terrain, the trajectory of biotechnology will undoubtedly reshape our approach to health, ethics, and the very essence of human identity. The dialogue between technological possibilities and ethical responsibilities continues to shape this dynamic field, promising a future where the boundaries of science extend into new realms of discovery and challenge.

1.6 The Internet of Things (IoT): Connecting the World One Device at a Time

Definition and Scope

The Internet of Things (IoT) represents a profound shift in the way we interact with technology, where the physical and digital worlds converge through a myriad of connected devices. At its core, IoT refers to the network of physical objects—'things'—that are embedded with sensors, software, and other technologies to connect and exchange data with other devices and systems over the internet. These devices range from ordinary household items like refrigerators and thermostats to sophisticated industrial tools. This network spans consumer, enterprise, and industrial spaces, each serving distinct purposes but together creating a tapestry of interconnected experiences that streamline processes and enhance the minutiae of daily life.

For instance, in the realm of home automation, IoT devices automate tasks traditionally done by humans—from adjusting lighting based on the time of day to heating your home before you arrive. In industrial settings, IoT becomes a powerful tool for optimizing manufacturing processes, enhancing supply chain management, and drastically improving safety measures. Such implementations demonstrate IoT's scope and versatility, reshaping industries and personal spaces with connectivity that was once the realm of science fiction.

Benefits and Applications

The applications of IoT are as diverse as they are impactful, permeating various sectors with the promise of enhanced efficiency, increased safety, and improved decision-making. In healthcare, IoT devices play a crucial role in the monitoring of chronic conditions; wearable devices that monitor heart rates, blood sugar levels, and other vital signs can transmit this data in real-time to healthcare providers, allowing for immediate responses to potential health issues. This not only revolutionizes patient care, but also significantly reduces the burdens on healthcare systems.

Agriculture too reaps the benefits of IoT technologies through precision farming—where farmers use IoT sensors to monitor soil moisture levels, crop growth, and livestock conditions, making informed decisions that enhance productivity and sustainability. These sensors provide data that help in optimizing water use, determining more effective planting strategies, and managing resources more efficiently, thus supporting sustainable agricultural practices.

In manufacturing, IoT connects machines and devices across production lines, enabling a seamless flow of information and a high level of operational efficiency. This integration allows for real-time monitoring and maintenance predictions, minimizing downtime and extending the lifespan of machinery. The result is a significant reduction in operational costs and an increase in production efficiency.

Security Challenges

However, the expansion of IoT also introduces significant security challenges, primarily related to data privacy and network security. Each connected device presents a potential entry point for security breaches, and the vast amount of data these devices collect and transmit can be highly sensitive—whether on personal health information, financial data, or critical infrastructure details.

The decentralized nature of IoT networks complicates the implementation of traditional security measures, which are often designed for centralized architectures. Therefore, securing an IoT network requires robust security protocols and continuous monitoring to prevent unauthorized access and to ensure data integrity. As IoT devices become more prevalent, the need for advanced security solutions, including end-to-end encryption, automated security updates, and advanced anomaly detection systems, becomes increasingly critical.

Future Trends

Looking to the future, IoT is set to become even more integrated into daily life and industrial processes. The convergence of IoT with other transformative technologies like artificial intelligence (AI) and machine learning (ML) heralds a new era of 'smart' solutions—where devices collect data and learn from it to make autonomous decisions. For urban planning and the development of smart cities, this integration promises optimized traffic systems, more efficient waste management, and enhanced energy distribution, fundamentally transforming urban environments into more sustainable, livable spaces.

The advent of 5G technology is poised to dramatically increase the speed and responsiveness of IoT devices, enabling more complex applications and a higher degree of interconnectivity. As these technologies continue to evolve, the potential of IoT to support a vast array of industries and activities will only expand, underscoring its role as a cornerstone of modern technological advancement.

As we navigate through this interconnected world, the potential of IoT to streamline enterprise operations, enhance everyday conveniences, and tackle substantial challenges like climate change is immense. However, this potential comes with the responsibility to address the inherent risks associated with increased connectivity, particularly those related to security and privacy. The future of IoT, while promising, demands careful consideration of these challenges as we move towards an increasingly connected society.

1.7 Virtual and Augmented Reality: Reshaping Entertainment and Education

Technology Overview

Virtual Reality (VR) and Augmented Reality (AR) are two facets of immersive technologies that have begun to alter the fabric of our interaction with the digital world, each distinct yet complementary in their functionality and application. VR immerses users in a completely virtual environment that is typically experienced via a head-mounted display (HMD) or through a specially designed space equipped with sensory components. This technology creates a controlled environment, manipulating the auditory and visual senses to transport users to entirely different realities, from simulated landscapes to fantastical worlds.

In contrast, AR overlays digital information onto the real world, enhancing one's perception of reality rather than replacing it.

Through devices such as smartphones, tablets, or even specialized AR glasses, users can see the world around them supplemented by digital data; for instance, a mechanic might see a motor's schematic overlaid directly on the piece of equipment they are repairing. The key to AR's functionality lies in its ability to anchor digital objects to the physical world in real-time, creating interactive experiences that blend reality with digital enhancements seamlessly.

Both VR and AR operate on the cutting edge of human-computer interaction, leveraging advanced graphics, real-time processing, and accurate environmental mapping to create immersive experiences. Their growth is propelled by significant advancements in sensor technology, computer vision, and graphics processing, which collectively enhance the fidelity and fluidity of the virtual and augmented experiences.

Impact on Entertainment

The entertainment industry, known for its quick adoption of innovative technologies, has been transformed by VR and AR, creating new paradigms for content delivery and consumption. In gaming, VR has introduced an unprecedented level of immersion, allowing players to step inside game worlds in a literal sense. Titles like 'Beat Saber' and 'Half-Life: Alyx' have set high standards for what immersive gaming can look and feel like, offering experiences that are both physically engaging and visually spectacular. The tactile feedback and 360-degree exploration capabilities in VR gaming deepen the sense of presence, making each session uniquely absorbing.

AR, while less immersive, offers more widespread applications in entertainment, particularly through mobile devices. Pokémon GO is a prime example, having blended AR with geolocation back in 2016 to create a gaming phenomenon that had millions venturing outdoors to catch virtual creatures superimposed on their real-world surroundings. Beyond gaming, AR is revolutionizing the film and tourism industries by providing enriched, interactive experiences. Tourists visiting historical sites, for example, can use AR applications to see reconstructions of ancient civilizations layered over present-day ruins, enhancing educational and cultural engagement without altering the physical site.

Educational Applications

The implications of VR and AR in education are profound, offering novel ways to engage students and enhance their learning experiences. VR's capability to create immersive educational environments allows students to experience historical events, distant locations, and complex scientific concepts firsthand. For instance, students can virtually visit the surface of Mars, explore the human anatomy in 3D, or step back in time to witness historical events. This level of immersion proves invaluable in subjects that benefit from experiential learning, making abstract or difficult concepts more accessible and engaging.

AR adds an interactive layer to education, turning classrooms into dynamic learning environments. Through AR, educational content can be superimposed onto the students' physical surroundings, bringing textbooks to life and allowing students to interact with educational material in a tangible way. This is particularly effective in science education, where complex processes, like the water cycle, can be visualized and manipulated in real-time, fostering a deeper understanding and retention of the subject matter.

Future Prospects

The future of VR and AR is poised for expansive growth, with potential applications extending far beyond entertainment and education into fields like healthcare, real estate, and manufacturing. In healthcare, VR is already being used for surgical training, providing a risk-free environment for surgeons to hone their skills. The next developments could see VR used more extensively for therapeutic purposes, where simulated environments are used to treat conditions such as PTSD or anxiety. AR could revolutionize patient care by providing surgeons with real-time, overlayed information during procedures, increasing precision and reducing risk.

In real estate, VR allows potential buyers to tour properties virtually, offering a convenient and comprehensive way to view homes without physical travel. AR could further enhance this by allowing viewers to customize and interact with space, changing furnishings and decor at the touch of a button. The integration of these technologies into everyday life is imminent, with the only real barriers being the refinement of the technologies and the reduction of costs associated with their implementation.

As these immersive technologies continue to evolve, their influence across various sectors is expected to grow, reshaping how we interact with the world and each other. The intersection of VR and AR with other technologies such as AI and IoT promises a future where the lines between digital and physical spaces become increasingly blurred, creating more cohesive, intuitive, and enhanced experiences. The ongoing development and integration of VR and AR technologies stand to transform existing industries and create entirely new realms of possibility in the digital age.

Chapter 2:
Ethical Dimensions of Modern Tech

As we venture deeper into the realms of modern technology, the ethical implications of our digital advancements become increasingly complex and intertwined with our daily lives. The rapid progression of artificial intelligence (AI) technologies, while offering profound benefits, also poses significant ethical dilemmas that demand careful consideration and proactive management. This chapter delves into the moral landscape of smart technology, focusing on AI as a pivotal element in the ongoing dialogue about the responsible use of powerful technological tools. As you navigate through this exploration, you are invited to reflect on the delicate balance between the benefits of AI and the ethical responsibilities it entails.

2.1 AI and Ethics: Navigating the Moral Landscape of Smart Technology

Bias and Fairness

The issue of bias in AI algorithms is one of the most pervasive ethical concerns in the field of artificial intelligence. Bias in AI typically originates from the data used to train these systems; if the data is skewed, the AI's decisions will likely be biased as well. This is particularly problematic in applications such as facial recognition systems and hiring algorithms, where biased AI can lead to unfair treatment of certain groups. For example, there have been instances where facial recognition technology has shown higher error rates for individuals of certain ethnic backgrounds due to underrepresentation in training datasets.

To mitigate bias and ensure fairness, strategies such as diversifying training data, implementing robust pre-release testing, and continuous monitoring for biases post-deployment are essential. One effective approach is to involve multidisciplinary teams in the development of AI systems, ensuring that diverse perspectives are considered in the design and implementation phases. Additionally, developing AI with explainability in mind—where decisions made by AI systems can be understood and scrutinized by humans—is crucial for identifying and correcting biases.

Transparency and Accountability

Transparency in AI operations is essential to build trust and ensure accountability, especially in critical applications like healthcare and law enforcement. In healthcare, AI systems used for diagnosing diseases or recommending treatments must be transparent in their operations to allow for proper validation and trust among medical professionals and patients. In law enforcement, the use of AI in predictive policing must be scrutinized to prevent unjust practices and protect civil liberties.

Holding AI systems accountable involves establishing clear guidelines and regulations that dictate the responsible use of AI. This includes setting standards for transparency, such as requiring developers to disclose the design choices, data sources, and decision-making processes of AI systems. Moreover, implementing robust mechanisms for auditing and oversight is crucial to ensure these technologies do not violate ethical norms or legal standards.

Autonomy vs. Control

The debate over the autonomy granted to AI systems versus the need for human oversight is a critical ethical issue. Complete autonomy in AI could lead to unintended consequences if these systems make decisions without human input in scenarios they were not adequately designed to handle. Conversely, excessive human control could undermine the efficiencies and advancements that autonomous systems offer.

The key is to strike a balance where AI systems are designed to handle tasks that are well-suited for automation while ensuring that humans remain in the loop in critical decision-making processes. This approach is particularly important in areas such as autonomous vehicles and military AI, where human oversight can prevent potential harm and ensure ethical considerations are taken into account.

Future Governance

Looking ahead, the governance of AI development and deployment is a monumental task that requires international cooperation and a multidisciplinary approach. Potential frameworks for AI governance should include provisions for promoting global standards that ensure safety, privacy, and fairness. The establishment of international bodies to oversee AI development, similar to how the International Atomic Energy Agency monitors nuclear technology, could be a way forward.

These frameworks should also encourage the sharing of best practices and technologies among nations to ensure that the benefits of AI are accessible to all. Additionally, fostering public discussions and engaging with various stakeholders, from policymakers to the general public, can help in crafting regulations that reflect broad societal values and ethical principles.

The ethical dimensions of modern technology, particularly AI, present challenges that are as daunting as they are critical to our collective future. As these technologies continue to evolve and integrate into every facet of human life, the decisions we make now will shape the ethical landscape of tomorrow. These decisions must be guided by a commitment to fairness, transparency, and accountability, ensuring that AI serves as a force for good in society.

2.2 Privacy in the Age of Digital Surveillance

In an era where digital footprints are as ubiquitous as the devices that enable them, the advancement in surveillance technologies such as facial recognition and location tracking has significantly transformed the landscape of personal privacy. Facial recognition technology, initially developed for security and authentication purposes, now pervades various sectors, from law enforcement to retail environments, analyzing features from images and videos to identify individuals. Similarly, location tracking, which utilizes GPS and other signals to pinpoint and record the position of devices, has become a standard functionality in many applications, ostensibly designed to enhance user convenience and safety.

These technologies, while beneficial, raise substantial privacy concerns. The capability to track an individual's movements or identify someone from a crowd without their consent encroaches on personal freedoms and anonymity. The use of facial recognition by law enforcement agencies, for example, has sparked debates over privacy rights versus public safety. Instances, where such technology is employed without clear regulatory frameworks or explicit consent from the individuals being surveilled, undermine trust in these systems and pose significant ethical dilemmas. Moreover, the accuracy of facial recognition systems has been called into question, with studies demonstrating disparities in the technology's ability to correctly identify individuals across different demographics, potentially leading to false identifications and unwarranted scrutiny.

The practices of data collection by corporations and governments exemplify the thin line between beneficial data gathering and the potential invasion of privacy. For corporations, the collection of consumer data underpins targeted advertising strategies and personalized services, driving economic benefits through enhanced customer experiences. However, when such data harvesting becomes opaque or overly intrusive, it shifts from being a service enhancement to a potential violation of privacy. Governments, under the guise of national security or public health, may also engage in extensive data surveillance practices. While such measures can aid in important functions like crime prevention or epidemiological tracking, they must be carefully balanced against the rights to privacy and personal autonomy, ensuring that such surveillance does not devolve into a tool for unwarranted social control.

Turning to consumer rights and protections, several laws and regulations have been established to safeguard personal privacy in the digital realm. The General Data Protection Regulation (GDPR) in Europe, for instance, sets a benchmark for privacy and data protection by enforcing strict guidelines on data handling and granting individuals substantial control over their data. This includes rights to access, correct, and delete personal information that organizations hold, as well as the requirement for clear consent before data collection. Similarly, the California Consumer Privacy Act (CCPA) empowers consumers with rights over their personal information collected by businesses, including the right to know about and decide how their data is used.

These regulations represent significant steps toward strengthening privacy protections, yet the enforcement and compliance with such laws remain challenging. The dynamic nature of technology and the international scope of the digital landscape often outpace regulatory frameworks, requiring ongoing adaptations and international cooperation to effectively protect privacy rights.

The challenges of maintaining anonymity online are further compounded by increasingly sophisticated data analysis techniques. In the digital age, the aggregation and analysis of data can reveal patterns and identities even when traditional identifiers are removed. Techniques such as data linking or de-anonymization, where disparate data sets are correlated to re-identify individuals, highlight the difficulties in achieving true anonymity. As data becomes an ever more valuable commodity, the techniques to mine and exploit it become more advanced, often outstripping the methods intended to obscure or protect personal identities.

Navigating this landscape requires not only robust legal frameworks and technologies designed to protect privacy, but also a cultural shift toward valuing and protecting personal data. Educating individuals about the implications of digital surveillance and the tools available for protecting privacy is crucial for empowering users to take control of their digital identities. As we continue to advance technologically, fostering a dialogue that prioritizes privacy and informed consent is essential for ensuring that surveillance technologies are employed responsibly and ethically.

2.3 Cybersecurity Threats: Protecting Data in a Networked World

The digital age, while a testament to human ingenuity and a catalyst for global connectivity, also ushers in an era of unprecedented cybersecurity threats. The landscape of cybersecurity is marred by the increasing frequency and sophistication of cyber-attacks such as ransomware and phishing. These attacks disrupt the operations of businesses and threaten national security and infringe upon the privacy of millions of individuals. Ransomware, a type of malware that encrypts a victim's files and demands payment to restore access, has evolved significantly. Modern ransomware attacks are meticulously planned, targeting specific organizations for maximum impact and ransom potential. Phishing attacks, wherein attackers masquerade as trustworthy entities to lure victims into revealing sensitive information, have become increasingly sophisticated, leveraging social engineering to manipulate users effectively.

The consequences of these threats are profound. Beyond the immediate disruption and financial loss, the long-term damage to consumer trust and organizational reputation can be debilitating. In response, robust cybersecurity measures are vital not only for the protection of sensitive information but also for the preservation of trust in digital systems. Protection strategies must evolve in tandem with the threats they aim to counter. For individuals, basic practices such as regular software updates, the use of strong, unique passwords, and a heightened awareness of phishing techniques are fundamental. However, as threats evolve, more sophisticated measures become necessary. Multifactor authentication (MFA), which requires multiple forms of verification before granting access, significantly enhances security by adding a layer of defense beyond mere passwords. Encryption, another critical strategy, secures data by encoding it in such a way that only authorized parties can decode it, providing a robust shield against unauthorized access.

For corporations and governments, the stakes are even higher, necessitating a comprehensive approach to cybersecurity. This includes not only technological solutions but also organizational policies that foster a culture of security. Regular audits, employee training programs, and incident response plans are essential components of an effective cybersecurity strategy. Moreover, collaboration between public and private sectors can amplify efforts to safeguard digital ecosystems. Information sharing about threats and vulnerabilities, for instance, can help anticipate and mitigate potential attacks more effectively.

The impact of significant data breaches extends beyond the direct effects on the compromised organization. Consumers, whose personal information may have been exposed, face the risk of identity theft and financial fraud, consequences that can persist long after the initial breach. For businesses, a breach can result in substantial financial losses, including regulatory fines, legal fees, and costs associated with repairing the damage. The erosion of consumer trust can lead to decreased customer retention and difficulty in attracting new business, compounding the financial impact. Moreover, the reputation of a company can suffer long-lasting damage, affecting its market position and competitive edge. Thus, the imperative to secure data is not solely a technical challenge but a fundamental aspect of business integrity and sustainability.

Looking to the future, the evolution of cybersecurity measures continues to intertwine with the advancements in technology, particularly with the integration of artificial intelligence (AI). AI presents a dual-edged sword in the realm of cybersecurity. On one hand, AI can significantly enhance defensive measures. Through the analysis of vast datasets, AI can identify patterns indicative of a cyber threat more efficiently than human analysts. AI-driven security systems can automate responses to threats in real-time, providing a dynamic defense mechanism that adapts as threats evolve. However, the use of AI also introduces new vulnerabilities. AI systems themselves can become targets of cyber-attacks, with hackers potentially manipulating AI algorithms to bypass security measures or even use AI to mount more effective attacks.

The ongoing challenge in cybersecurity is thus not only to defend against current threats but also to anticipate and prepare for future vulnerabilities. This dynamic field demands constant vigilance, innovation, and adaptability, qualities that must be ingrained in the strategies and cultures of all stakeholders involved in the digital ecosystem. As we continue to rely more on digital solutions across all aspects of society, the role of cybersecurity becomes increasingly central, not just as a technical requirement but as a foundational pillar of a secure and trustworthy digital future.

2.4 Ethical Implications of Genomic Data Usage

The unprecedented advancements in genomic technologies have ushered in an era where the manipulation and analysis of genetic data have become routine practices in medicine, research, and even consumer services. However, the collection and storage of genomic data raise substantial privacy concerns. The intimate nature of this data, which can reveal not just medical conditions but also potential risks and even familial connections, makes it a target for misuse. Unauthorized access to genomic databases can lead to scenarios where genetic information is used without individual consent, possibly for purposes that harm, discriminate, or infringe upon personal privacy. For example, if genomic data were accessed by malicious parties, it could lead to targeted scams or be used to tailor phishing attacks that exploit an individual's genetic health risks.

The potential for misuse underscores the need for stringent security measures and ethical guidelines to govern how genomic data is stored and accessed. Encryption of genetic data, secure databases, and rigorous access controls are essential to protect sensitive information from unauthorized access. Moreover, transparency in how genomic data is used and who has access to it is crucial for maintaining public trust. Individuals should be clearly informed about how their data will be used, who might have access, and the measures in place to protect their privacy. This level of transparency helps in building trust and empowers individuals to make informed decisions about participating in genetic testing or research.

Issues surrounding consent for genomic data use and the ongoing debate over data ownership and access rights further complicate the ethical landscape. Unlike other types of personal data, genomic information carries implications not just for the individual from whom it originates, but also for their biological relatives who may share similar genetic markers. This interconnectedness means that informed consent must cover not just the use of an individual's data but also the potential implications for family members. The consent process should be comprehensive and continuous, allowing individuals to understand and revisit their consent choices as new uses for genetic data evolve.

Ownership of genomic data is another contentious issue. While individuals have a clear stake in deciding how their genetic information is used, the data also holds significant value for research institutions, pharmaceutical companies, and healthcare providers who can use it to advance medical research and improve healthcare outcomes. Balancing these interests requires a model of data governance that recognizes both the rights of individuals to control their genetic information and the benefits of using this data for societal good. Developing frameworks that allow for the sharing of genetic data with safeguards to protect individual rights could facilitate this balance, promoting innovation while respecting privacy.

Discrimination based on genomic information is a significant risk, particularly in the realms of employment and insurance. Employers or insurers could potentially use genetic data to discriminate against individuals who are predisposed to certain conditions, denying them opportunities or coverage unfairly. Such discrimination violates individual rights and undermines the potential benefits of genomic medicine. Legal protections, similar to the Genetic Information Nondiscrimination Act (GINA) in the United States, are crucial to prevent genetic discrimination. These laws need to be robust and enforceable, ensuring that individuals feel safe to benefit from genetic testing and research without fear of discrimination.

Regulatory frameworks play a critical role in managing the ethical use of genomic data. Current regulations vary significantly across different countries, reflecting diverse cultural, ethical, and social values. To effectively address the challenges posed by genomic data, these frameworks must evolve to keep pace with technological advancements. Regulations should enforce strict standards for consent, privacy protection, security, and non-discrimination. Moreover, as genomic technologies transcend national boundaries, international cooperation becomes essential. Developing global standards and guidelines can help harmonize regulations, ensuring consistent protection for individuals regardless of where their data is stored or used.

Improvements to regulatory frameworks could include clearer guidelines on the use of de-identified or anonymized data, which is often used in research. While removing identifiers from genomic data can reduce privacy risks, the unique nature of genetic information means that re-identification is still a possibility. Regulations should address these risks, ensuring that even anonymized data is used in ways that respect individual privacy and consent. Additionally, engaging the public in discussions about genomic data use and its implications can help shape policies that reflect societal values and priorities, fostering a more inclusive approach to genomic governance.

As we continue to navigate the complexities of genomic data usage, it is clear that the challenges are as profound as the opportunities. Balancing the benefits of genomic research and medicine with the need to protect individual privacy and prevent discrimination requires a thoughtful approach to ethical governance and public engagement. By addressing these issues proactively, we can harness the power of genomics to improve health and society while safeguarding the rights and dignity of individuals.

2.5 Autonomous Tech: Responsibility and Regulation

As the curtain rises on the era of autonomous technologies, from self-driving vehicles to autonomous robotic systems, a complex web of ethical, legal, and social questions comes into focus. These technologies, while poised to revolutionize our daily lives, bring forth significant liability issues that challenge existing legal frameworks. In the realm of autonomous vehicles (AVs), for instance, the traditional notions of liability are turned on their head. Traditionally, in the event of a traffic accident, liability often rests with the human driver. However, with AVs, determining liability becomes more complicated if the vehicle itself can make decisions. This shift raises critical questions: If an autonomous vehicle is involved in an accident, who is at fault? Is it the manufacturer, the software developer, or the vehicle owner? Or is it the AI itself?

The resolution of these issues requires a rethinking of liability laws to accommodate the unique challenges posed by autonomous technologies. One approach could be the implementation of a no-fault insurance model, where damages are paid out regardless of who is at fault, thus avoiding lengthy litigation over liability. Alternatively, a new legal framework might allocate liability based on the level of control exerted by the human operator versus the autonomy of the technology. Such frameworks would necessitate a clear understanding of the various levels of vehicle autonomy, from partially automated systems that require human oversight to fully autonomous systems that operate without any human intervention.

The regulatory challenges associated with keeping pace with rapid technological advancements add another layer of complexity. Regulators find themselves in a perpetual catch-up game as technologies evolve faster than the policies designed to govern them. Creating effective policies that safeguard public safety without stifling innovation is a delicate balance. This challenge is compounded by the global nature of technology development, which often outpaces the jurisdictional boundaries of national regulatory bodies. International collaboration, therefore, becomes essential in developing harmonized standards and regulations that ensure safety and accountability while supporting cross-border compatibility of autonomous technologies.

Ethical deployment of autonomous technologies also prompts reflection on broader societal impacts, particularly concerning the potential displacement of jobs. As autonomous systems become capable of performing tasks traditionally done by humans, from driving trucks to managing supply chains, the risk of significant job displacement looms large. This shift affects those directly displaced and has ripple effects across economies and communities. It raises urgent questions about how society might adapt to such changes and how technology developers and policymakers can mitigate negative impacts. Solutions might include retraining programs to help displaced workers transition into new roles and the development of economic policies that support job creation in sectors likely to expand as a result of automation.

Building public trust and acceptance is crucial for the successful integration of autonomous technologies into society. Trust hinges on transparency and the responsible development of technologies. Clear communication about how autonomous systems work, the safety measures in place, and the handling of data privacy issues can help demystify these technologies for the public. Furthermore, involving the public in discussions about the deployment of autonomous technologies can foster a greater understanding and acceptance. Public trials, open forums for feedback, and transparent reporting of test results can all serve as avenues for engaging the public and building trust.

As we navigate these uncharted waters, the intersection of technology and regulation will undoubtedly continue to evolve. The journey toward integrating autonomous technologies into our lives is not just about technological achievement, but also about crafting the legal and ethical frameworks that will support their integration into society responsibly.

2.6 The Sustainability of Tech: Environmental Concerns of Modern Innovations

The relentless pace of technological innovation, while driving unprecedented progress, casts a substantial environmental shadow that cannot be ignored. As we delve into the sustainability of modern technologies, it becomes crucial to confront the environmental impacts associated with the lifecycle of tech products—from their creation to their eventual disposal. The extraction of rare earth elements, essential for the production of high-tech devices, poses significant environmental challenges. These elements, found in everything from smartphones to electric vehicles, are mined in processes that often lead to severe ecological damage, including soil erosion, water contamination, and deforestation. The mining and refining processes are not only energy-intensive but also release a wide array of pollutants that can cause long-term harm to ecosystems and communities.

Moreover, the end of the lifecycle of tech products brings additional environmental concerns. The disposal of electronic waste, or e-waste, is a growing problem globally. As technology cycles become shorter and consumer demand for the latest devices continues to rise, the volume of e-waste has skyrocketed, leading to significant health and environmental risks. Inadequately managed e-waste often ends up in landfills, where toxic substances such as lead, mercury, and cadmium can leach into the soil and water, posing serious health risks to nearby populations. Furthermore, the informal processing of e-waste, prevalent in several developing countries, exposes workers to hazardous conditions without adequate protection or health considerations.

To address these pressing issues, the development and adoption of sustainable disposal methods are paramount. Recycling and re-purposing e-waste can mitigate environmental harm and recover valuable materials that can be reused in the manufacturing of new products. Advanced recycling technologies that increase the efficiency and effectiveness of material recovery are critical to reducing the ecological footprint of e-waste. Additionally, promoting consumer awareness and involvement in recycling programs can help increase recycling rates and reduce the overall environmental impact of e-waste.

The energy consumption of technology, particularly in data centers, is another area of significant environmental impact. Data centers, crucial for storing, processing, and distributing large amounts of data, consume vast amounts of energy, contributing to the high carbon footprint associated with digital activities. The cooling systems, necessary to prevent overheating, add to the energy expenditure, making traditional data centers some of the most energy-intensive facilities globally. However, the shift towards greener and more sustainable energy sources offers a path forward. Innovations such as the use of renewable energy sources, energy-efficient cooling systems, and advanced server architectures can dramatically reduce the energy consumption and carbon emissions of data centers. Companies like Google and Microsoft have been leading the way, investing in renewable energy projects and aiming for carbon neutrality in their operations.

Innovations in green technology present promising solutions to the environmental challenges posed by the tech industry. Developments in battery technology, for example, are critical for enhancing the energy efficiency and sustainability of everything from consumer electronics to electric vehicles. New battery formulations and recycling technologies can extend battery life, reduce reliance on rare earth elements, and decrease environmental degradation associated with battery production and disposal. Similarly, advances in energy-efficient computing, from low-power hardware components to software optimizations, can significantly reduce the energy consumption of electronic devices and systems.

As we explore these innovations and their potential to mitigate the environmental impacts of technology, it becomes clear that the path to sustainability in the tech industry requires a concerted effort across multiple fronts. From reducing the resource consumption associated with production to enhancing the energy efficiency of operations and improving e-waste management, each step forward contributes to a more sustainable technological ecosystem. This holistic approach addresses the immediate environmental challenges and paves the way for a future where technology and sustainability are inextricably linked, ensuring that our technological advances do not come at the expense of our planet.

In summarizing the main points of this exploration into the sustainability of technology, we recognize the dual aspects of modern innovations: their capacity to drive progress and their potential to impart environmental costs. The balance we seek between these aspects is not merely a technical challenge but a profound responsibility that calls for innovation, regulation, and awareness. As we transition into the next chapter, which delves deeper into the social implications of technological integration into our daily lives, let us carry forward the understanding that sustainability must be a cornerstone of all future technological advancements, ensuring that our strides in innovation are matched by our commitments to environmental stewardship.

Chapter 3:
Technology in Everyday Life

As we navigate the corridors of our daily lives, the silent whispers of technology echo around us, subtly yet profoundly shaping our domestic landscapes. The digital revolution, once confined to the realms of academia and industry, now permeates the sanctity of our homes, promising a future where living spaces are not just shelters but intelligent environments that respond to our needs, learn our preferences, and anticipate our desires. This chapter explores how the integration of technology in home environments is transforming mundane domestic routines into enriched experiences that blend convenience, security, and sustainability into the fabric of everyday life.

3.1 Smart Homes and the Future of Living Spaces

The concept of a 'smart home' is no longer a futuristic fantasy; it has evolved into a tangible reality, enabled by the Internet of Things (IoT). Imagine your home as a symphony, where each appliance, from refrigerators to lighting systems, plays an instrument. The conductor of this symphony is IoT technology, which enables these devices to communicate and coordinate with each other seamlessly, creating a harmonious environment tailored to your preferences and routines.

Integration of IoT Devices

The integration of IoT devices in homes has redefined the concept of living spaces. These devices, equipped with sensors and connected via the internet, can monitor various aspects of the home environment and automate tasks to enhance convenience and energy efficiency. For example, smart thermostats learn your temperature preferences and adjust the heating or cooling systems based on when you are home, significantly reducing energy consumption. Similarly, smart refrigerators can keep track of your groceries, suggest recipes based on the ingredients available, and even order groceries when you are running low. This level of automation simplifies household management and enhances the efficiency of daily chores, allowing you more time to focus on what truly matters.

Voice-Activated Assistants

Voice-activated assistants, such as Amazon Alexa, Google Assistant, and Apple Siri, have become the cornerstone of user interaction within smart homes. These AI-driven assistants process natural language to perform tasks ranging from setting reminders and playing music to controlling smart devices throughout the home. The convenience of voice commands simplifies the management of your home environment, making technology accessible to everyone, regardless of their technical expertise. Whether you are cooking and need a quick recipe suggestion or want to control the lighting without leaving your cozy bed, these assistants make it possible with just a few spoken words.

Security Innovations

As homes become smarter, security technologies have also advanced to protect against intrusions and ensure the safety of residents. Smart locks and surveillance systems, enhanced with facial recognition and real-time alerts, provide peace of mind by offering robust security solutions that are both proactive and reactive. Smart locks can be controlled remotely, allowing you to grant access to visitors without needing a physical key. Integrated surveillance systems can detect unusual activity and immediately alert you on your smartphone, providing real-time security monitoring. These systems deter potential intruders and allow you to monitor your home remotely, ensuring that your sanctuary remains protected at all times.

Future Trends in Home Automation

Looking towards the horizon, the future of home automation holds promising developments that could further integrate technology into our living spaces. AI-powered domestic robots, for instance, are on the cusp of becoming household staples. These robots could handle everything from cleaning and maintenance to providing companionship, fundamentally transforming household dynamics. Additionally, the continued integration of smart appliances could lead to fully autonomous kitchens that prepare meals before you even think of what you'd like to eat. Imagine a scenario where your home anticipates your needs and adapts its environment to optimize your comfort and productivity throughout the day.

The evolution of smart homes reflects a broader trend towards more integrated, personalized, and adaptive technological environments. As we continue to embrace these innovations, our living spaces will become more responsive, effectively becoming extensions of our preferences and behaviors. The potential to enhance convenience, efficiency, and security in our homes is immense, promising a future where technology enriches our daily lives in the most intimate of spaces.

3.2 Wearable Technology: Health Monitoring and Beyond

In the intricate dance of daily life, where every step and heartbeat carries information crucial to our well-being, wearable technology emerges as a pivotal player. This technology, once limited to the realms of fitness bands and step counters, has evolved into sophisticated devices capable of monitoring a wide array of vital signs and physical activities. These wearables, worn on the wrist, embedded in clothing, or even ingeniously integrated into accessories like rings and watches, do more than just count steps or measure heartbeats; they provide a continuous stream of health data that contributes significantly to preventative healthcare and personalized fitness regimes.

Devices equipped with sensors to monitor heart rates, sleep patterns, and even blood oxygen levels offer insights that were once only available in clinical settings. For instance, consider a wearable device that not only tracks your heart rate during various activities but also notices irregular heart rhythms and alerts you to potential health issues before they become critical. This proactive health monitoring can guide users to seek medical advice early, potentially preventing severe conditions from developing. Furthermore, these devices often come with applications that analyze the collected data over time, allowing you to observe trends and patterns in your physical activity and health status, thereby promoting a healthier lifestyle tailored to your personal needs.

Beyond the sphere of fitness and everyday health monitoring, wearable technology has begun paving its way into more advanced medical diagnostics. Wearable devices equipped with specialized sensors can continuously monitor conditions such as diabetes by tracking glucose levels non-invasively. This constant monitoring not only helps in managing the condition more effectively but also reduces the need for frequent, painful blood tests. Similarly, for patients with cardiovascular diseases, wearable devices can monitor heart function and detect abnormalities that might require urgent medical attention. The data collected by these devices can be invaluable not only for the wearer but also for their healthcare providers, offering a more comprehensive view of the patient's condition than what can be observed during occasional clinic visits.

The integration of wearable technology into daily life goes beyond health and fitness. These devices enhance user convenience by supporting various day-to-day tasks through connectivity features. Wearable devices can now process payments, replacing the need for cash or cards with a simple tap of a wrist at the checkout. Navigation is another area where wearables offer significant advantages; with GPS-enabled devices, directions can be given directly through the wearable, allowing for more convenient and less obtrusive guidance than ever before. This seamless integration of technology into everyday activities simplifies tasks and enhances the efficiency of our daily routines, allowing for a smoother, more connected day-to-day experience.

Looking to the future, the prospects for wearable technology are boundless. The potential integration with virtual reality (VR) offers exciting possibilities for both entertainment and training simulations, providing a more immersive experience that could revolutionize how we interact with digital content. In mental health treatment, wearables could play a transformative role by aiding in the monitoring and management of conditions such as anxiety and depression. Imagine a device that tracks stress levels via physiological signals and provides real-time interventions, such as guided breathing exercises or mood-enhancing activities, tailored to the wearer's emotional state. This could empower individuals to manage their mental health more proactively, with personalized tools at their fingertips.

As we continue to weave technology more deeply into the fabric of our lives, wearable devices stand at the forefront of this integration, offering tools that enhance our health, streamline our tasks, and expand our horizons. The evolution of wearable technology promises not only enhanced functionality but also a deeper connection to our own bodies and environments, heralding a future where our very well-being is continuously supported by the technology we wear.

3.3 How AI is Transforming Customer Service Industries

The landscape of customer service has been fundamentally reshaped by the advent and integration of artificial intelligence (AI), propelling a shift towards more dynamic, responsive, and personalized customer interactions. AI-driven technologies, such as chatbots and virtual assistants, have not only streamlined operations but have also redefined the nature of customer engagement, offering new avenues for enhancing service delivery and customer satisfaction. The deployment of these AI tools across various customer service platforms reflects a broader trend toward automating and optimizing service processes, where AI's capability to analyze vast amounts of data in real-time translates into more efficient and effective service solutions.

Chatbots and Virtual Assistants

AI-driven chatbots and virtual assistants represent a significant evolution in the way businesses interact with their customers. By leveraging natural language processing (NLP) and machine learning algorithms, these tools can understand and respond to customer inquiries with increasing accuracy. Unlike traditional customer service channels that often require human intervention, AI-enabled chatbots provide instant responses to customer queries, reducing wait times and improving overall service efficiency. For instance, a customer looking for product information or troubleshooting advice can receive immediate assistance from a chatbot, which can access a vast database of knowledge and deliver accurate information in seconds. Moreover, these AI-driven systems are capable of learning from each interaction, continuously improving their responses, and adapting to new queries, which makes them increasingly reliable and effective over time.

This capability not only enhances customer satisfaction by providing quick and accurate information but also allows human customer service representatives to focus on more complex and nuanced issues, thereby optimizing workforce efficiency and effectiveness. Additionally, virtual assistants are now an integral part of many e-commerce platforms, guiding customers through the shopping experience with personalized suggestions and offers based on their browsing and purchase history. This level of personalized interaction enhances the customer experience and drives sales and customer loyalty by making shopping more engaging and tailored to individual preferences.

Personalization of Services

One of the most significant impacts of AI in customer service is the ability to personalize interactions at scale. AI systems analyze customer data, including past purchases, browsing behaviors, and preferences, to tailor services and recommendations specifically to individual needs. This personalization extends beyond simple product recommendations; it encompasses the entire service experience, from customized marketing messages to individualized shopping experiences, and even personalized customer support. For example, an AI system might analyze a customer's purchase history and suggest complementary products, or it might offer troubleshooting tips based on the specific issues a customer has encountered in the past.

This deep level of personalization not only improves customer satisfaction by making interactions more relevant and targeted but also enhances the efficiency of marketing and sales strategies by focusing resources on the opportunities most likely to convert. Furthermore, by automating the personalization process, businesses can achieve a level of individual attention that would be impossible to replicate with a human workforce alone. This scalability of personalized service is a key advantage of AI in customer service, allowing businesses to meet the expectations of their customers more effectively and efficiently.

Operational Efficiency

AI also plays a crucial role in enhancing operational efficiency within customer service departments. Through the automation of routine tasks such as ticket sorting, issue categorization, and basic customer queries, AI frees up human agents to handle more complex and sensitive issues, thereby optimizing the allocation of human resources. Additionally, AI-driven predictive maintenance can anticipate issues before they occur, reducing downtime and maintaining service continuity. For example, in a telecommunications company, AI can predict when specific components are likely to fail and schedule preventive maintenance, thus avoiding service disruptions that could impact large numbers of customers.

Moreover, AI analytics can provide managers with in-depth insights into customer service operations, identifying patterns and trends that can help improve service strategies and operations. These insights can lead to more informed decision-making and better resource management, further enhancing the efficiency and effectiveness of customer service departments.

Challenges and Opportunities

Despite the numerous benefits, the integration of AI in customer service also presents several challenges. Privacy concerns are at the forefront, as the use of AI involves the collection, analysis, and storage of vast amounts of personal customer data. Ensuring the security of this data and maintaining customer trust requires robust data protection measures and transparent privacy policies. Additionally, the risk of over-reliance on AI solutions can lead to a depersonalization of customer interactions, where customers feel disconnected from the human element of service. Balancing AI automation with human empathy and understanding is crucial to maintaining a positive customer experience.

Furthermore, as AI technologies continue to evolve, there are significant opportunities for growth and innovation in customer service. The integration of advanced AI capabilities, such as emotional recognition, could further enhance the understanding and responsiveness of AI systems, allowing for more nuanced and empathetic interactions. The ongoing development of AI in customer service holds the promise of more innovative, efficient, and personalized customer experiences, offering a competitive edge to businesses that successfully integrate these technologies into their service operations.

As we continue to explore the assorted impacts of AI across various industries, the realm of customer service stands out as a prime example of how technology can enhance human capabilities and redefine traditional business practices. The journey of integrating AI into customer service is an ongoing process of balancing benefits and challenges, a testament to the complex interplay between technology, business, and the ever-evolving expectations of customers.

3.4 Drones in Agriculture: A Leap Towards Sustainable Farming

In the vast expanses of modern agriculture, where the health of every crop and the efficiency of every process can tip the scales between abundance and scarcity, drones have soared to the forefront as pivotal tools for innovation. Precision agriculture, a practice that melds technology with farming techniques to increase efficiency and reduce waste, has found a dynamic ally in drones. These unmanned aerial vehicles (UAVs) are revolutionizing the way farmland is managed, providing farmers with detailed insights that were once costly or impossible to obtain.

Precision Agriculture

Drones equipped with advanced imaging technology enable precise monitoring of crop health across extensive fields, transforming the landscape of agricultural management. By capturing high-resolution images and leveraging spectral imaging, drones can identify areas of stress in crops long before problems become visible to the naked eye. This capability allows for the early detection of issues such as nutrient deficiencies, water stress, and pest infestations, facilitating timely interventions that can stave off potential losses. Moreover, drones optimize water usage by providing precise data on the moisture levels of soil across different parts of a farm. This information enables farmers to implement variable-rate irrigation systems where water distribution can be tailored to the specific needs of different sections, thus conserving water—a resource as precious as the crops it nurtures.

The integration of drones into daily farming operations enhances the precision of agricultural practices and boosts sustainability. With better data on crop health and soil conditions, farmers can reduce the overuse of fertilizers and pesticides, minimizing runoff and the environmental impact associated with traditional farming methods. This shift not only aligns with global efforts toward environmental conservation but also supports the economic stability of farming operations by reducing unnecessary expenses.

Data Collection and Analysis

The value of drones extends beyond mere observation; their true potential lies in their ability to collect and analyze data, transforming raw information into actionable insights. Drones can be equipped with various sensors, including thermal, hyperspectral, and multispectral sensors, which collect data that is vital for making informed decisions about crop management. This data is then processed using sophisticated algorithms that can map out trends and patterns over time, providing farmers with a comprehensive understanding of their fields.

This analytical capability enables more than just problem detection. It supports strategic decision-making about planting and crop rotation, which can significantly influence yield outcomes. For instance, data collected by drones can help determine the optimal planting density and arrangements, which vary depending on crop type and local soil and weather conditions. Furthermore, insights into the growth patterns and health of crops throughout the season allow farmers to plan more effective harvesting schedules, ensuring that each crop is picked at its peak.

Pesticide and Fertilizer Application

Drones also play a crucial role in the precise application of pesticides and fertilizers, reducing farming's environmental footprint. Equipped with advanced dispensing systems, drones can target specific areas that require treatment, minimizing the volume of chemicals used. This targeted approach not only reduces the cost associated with pesticide and fertilizer use but also lessens the environmental impact, preventing the over-application that can lead to harmful runoff and soil degradation.

Moreover, the ability of drones to access areas that are difficult for traditional machinery to reach, such as steep terrains or densely planted fields, ensures that no part of the farm is neglected. This comprehensive coverage helps maintain the health and productivity of every crop, which is essential for the sustainability of the farm.

Future of Farming Technologies

Looking to the future, the role of drones in agriculture is set to expand as technology advances. The integration of AI with drone technology promises even smarter agricultural practices, where drones can autonomously monitor, diagnose, and treat crop issues without human intervention. Imagine drones that detect a pest infestation, calculate the optimal mix and quantity of pesticides needed, and apply them, all without a farmer needing to set foot in the field.

Additionally, the ongoing advancements in battery technology and drone design are expected to lead to longer flight times and better payload capacities, allowing for more extensive and frequent coverage of farmland. This progression will likely make drones an indispensable tool for farmers around the world, further entrenching technology's role in agriculture.

As we continue to face global challenges such as climate change and population growth, the importance of sustainable and efficient farming practices becomes increasingly clear. Drones, with their ability to enhance the precision, efficiency, and sustainability of farming, are at the forefront of this agricultural evolution. Embracing this technology supports the economic goals of farmers and contributes to a broader vision of environmental stewardship and food security. As we advance, the skies above our farms will likely buzz with the sound of drones, a testament to technology's role in nurturing the earth's bounty.

3.5 Educational Technologies and Remote Learning: The New Classroom

The transformation of the educational landscape through technology has not only revolutionized the method and medium of instruction but has fundamentally altered the way students engage and interact with educational content. Interactive whiteboards and student response systems are just the tip of the iceberg in a wide array of technologies that are enhancing student engagement in both physical classrooms and virtual learning environments. Interactive whiteboards, for example, allow for dynamic presentations where teachers can annotate directly on the display, connect various multimedia resources, and even share screens with students, making the learning experience much more engaging compared to traditional blackboard-based teaching. This visual and interactive approach quantifies learning, making complex subjects more accessible and understandable to students of all ages.

Moreover, student response systems have transformed the traditional classroom dynamic, fostering a more interactive and participatory learning environment. These systems allow students to answer quizzes, participate in polls, and provide feedback in real-time using clickers or mobile apps. This immediate interaction keeps students engaged and allows educators to gauge understanding and adjust their teaching strategies on the fly, ensuring that all students are keeping pace with the lesson. The data collected through these responses can also be used to provide personalized feedback to students, further enhancing their learning experience.

The role of technology in providing greater accessibility and inclusivity in education is particularly noteworthy. Advanced educational technologies have opened doors for students who might otherwise find learning environments inaccessible. Online learning platforms, for instance, offer courses with adjustable learning paces, subtitles, sign language interpretation, and customizable learning paths that cater to the needs of students with disabilities. These platforms ensure that education is not a privilege of the few but a universal right accessible to all, regardless of physical, geographical, or socio-economic barriers. This democratization of education broadens educational opportunities for individuals and enriches the learning community with a diversity of perspectives and experiences.

The rise of remote learning platforms has been one of the most significant educational phenomena lately, particularly highlighted by the global shift to online learning during the COVID-19 pandemic. Platforms such as Zoom, Microsoft Teams, and Google Classroom have become integral to continuing education in times of disruption. These platforms enable not just video conferencing but also integrate tools for assignment distribution, discussion forums, and collaborative projects, thereby maintaining the continuity of education even in the most challenging circumstances. The scalability of these platforms means that institutions can offer education not just to students in local geography but to a global audience, thus expanding their reach and impact.

However, the integration of technology in education is not without its challenges. The digital divide—the gap between those who have access to modern information and communication technology and those who do not—is a significant barrier. Students in rural areas or from lower socio-economic backgrounds may not have access to reliable internet or the devices necessary to participate in digital learning, which can widen educational inequalities. Furthermore, there is the issue of information overload and digital distraction, where the vast resources available online can overwhelm students, detracting from focused learning.

Predicting the evolution of educational technology, it is clear that edtech is not a mere trend but a fundamental shift in how education is delivered and experienced. Future advancements are likely to include greater integration of artificial intelligence, which can tailor educational content to individual learning styles and needs, making learning even more personalized and effective. Virtual and augmented reality technologies could make experiential learning more mainstream, providing students with immersive experiences that enhance understanding and retention of knowledge. As we continue to navigate these changes, the potential of educational technology to transform learning is boundless, promising a future where education is more engaging, inclusive, and accessible than ever before. The ongoing challenge for educators, policymakers, and technologists is to harness these tools in ways that address existing inequalities and enhance the educational experience without overwhelming the very individuals they seek to empower.

3.6 The Impact of Social Media on Digital Communication

In the tapestry of modern connectivity, social media platforms stand out as vibrant threads, intricately woven into the daily routines of billions globally. These platforms have not merely changed how people communicate; they have redefined the very essence of community building and relationship maintenance. As you scroll through your feeds, consider how these digital realms have become pivotal in fostering connections that bridge geographical, cultural, and societal divides. Social media platforms like Facebook, Twitter, and Instagram offer more than just spaces for sharing photos and updates; they facilitate the formation of communities around common interests, causes, and passions. Whether it is groups dedicated to hobbies, support networks for health issues, or forums for political activism, these platforms enable individuals to find and connect with like-minded people, regardless of physical distance.

The role of social media in community building is complemented by its capacity to maintain and strengthen relationships. Features such as instant messaging, video calls, and timeline updates help keep friends and families connected, sharing in life's moments, both big and small. The ease and immediacy of these interactions support a continuous sharing of experiences, thoughts, and emotions, fostering relationships that might otherwise have dwindled due to the constraints of time and space. This digital connectivity does more than just keep existing relationships alive; it enhances them, allowing for more frequent and varied exchange of support, love, and understanding.

Beyond personal relationships and community building, social media wields significant influence over public opinion, shaping political and social discourse on a scale previously unimaginable. Platforms like Twitter have become arenas for political debate, places where policies are discussed, critiqued, and promoted. Moreover, social media has the power to mobilize public opinion quickly, organizing collective actions such as protests or charity drives with incredible speed and efficiency. However, the influence of social media on public opinion is a double-edged sword. While it democratizes information, offering a platform for voices that might otherwise go unheard, it also opens the door to misinformation and manipulation. The viral nature of social media can amplify not just truths but also falsehoods, leading to significant real-world consequences, as seen in various political upheavals around the world.

Turning to the realm of commerce, social media has emerged as a formidable tool for marketing and business. The interactive nature of these platforms allows businesses to engage directly with consumers, creating relationships that foster brand loyalty and customer retention. Social media marketing strategies often involve content that is engaging, relatable, and sharable, extending brand reach through organic interactions. Influencer marketing, where businesses collaborate with social media personalities who have large followings, exemplifies this trend. These influencers can sway public opinion about products and brands more effectively than traditional advertising, leveraging their authenticity and relatability to influence purchasing decisions.

However, the commercial use of social media is not without its challenges. The line between genuine content and advertising is often blurred, leading to potential distrust among consumers. Moreover, the reliance on algorithms to deliver personalized content can lead to echo chambers where users see only what aligns with their views or interests, potentially limiting exposure to new ideas and diverse perspectives. This algorithmic curation, while effective for keeping users engaged with the platform, raises ethical concerns about privacy and the psychological effects of such targeted content.

As we look to the future of social media, anticipating its trajectory involves acknowledging both its vast potential and its significant challenges. The evolution of these platforms will likely see greater integration of augmented reality (AR) and virtual reality (VR), offering even more immersive and engaging ways to connect and interact. This could redefine social interactions, creating spaces that are more vivid and interactive than ever before. However, as these technologies develop, so too do the ethical considerations they bring, particularly concerning data privacy and the management of virtual interactions. The ongoing debate over the responsibility of social media companies in monitoring and managing content will also continue to shape the landscape. Balancing freedom of expression with the need to prevent harm, whether through misinformation, cyberbullying, or other forms of abuse, remains a critical challenge.

Navigating these complexities requires a nuanced understanding of both the technology and the human behaviors it influences. As social media continues to evolve, it remains a mirror reflecting our societies, magnifying both our virtues and our flaws. Its role in digital communication is undeniably profound, shaping not just how we connect with others but also how we see the world and ourselves within it. As we engage with these platforms, we must be mindful of the influence they wield and the responsibilities they entail, both for users and creators alike.

3.7 E-commerce Evolution: AI and Personalization Trends

In the dynamic world of e-commerce, artificial intelligence (AI) has emerged as a transformative force, redefining the shopping experience by infusing it with unprecedented levels of personalization and efficiency. As you navigate through online shopping platforms, AI silently works in the background, analyzing your behavior, predicting your preferences, and personalizing every interaction to suit your unique tastes and needs. This evolution of e-commerce is not just about selling products; it's about creating a shopping experience that feels intuitive, effortless, and distinctly tailored to each individual.

AI technologies such as machine learning and predictive analytics revolutionize e-commerce by enabling platforms to offer highly personalized experiences that drive engagement and sales. Machine learning algorithms analyze vast amounts of data from user interactions, such as page views, purchase history, and search queries, to identify patterns and preferences. These insights allow e-commerce platforms to recommend products that you are more likely to purchase, even before you realize you need them. For instance, if you have been browsing for books within a specific genre, AI can suggest new releases or undiscovered titles, creating a sense of discovery and personalized curation. Additionally, predictive analytics can forecast future buying behavior by identifying trends and seasonal demands, ensuring that e-commerce platforms are always one step ahead in meeting consumer expectations.

The ability of AI to enhance user experience extends beyond mere product recommendations. It profoundly impacts inventory management and marketing strategies by providing insights that are precisely aligned with consumer behavior. E-commerce businesses can optimize their stock levels based on predictive models that anticipate which products will be in high demand, thereby reducing overstock and understock scenarios. This not only minimizes waste but also ensures that popular items are readily available, enhancing customer satisfaction. Furthermore, AI-driven insights enable marketers to design targeted campaigns that resonate with specific demographics, increasing the effectiveness of marketing efforts and maximizing return on investment.

The integration of e-commerce with other cutting-edge technologies like augmented reality (AR) and blockchain opens new vistas for innovation. AR transforms the online shopping experience by allowing you to visualize products in your environment before making a purchase. For example, you can see how a piece of furniture would look in your living room or how a pair of sunglasses fit your face, bridging the gap between the digital and physical worlds. This immersive interaction not only aids in making more informed purchase decisions but also significantly enhances user engagement, reducing the likelihood of returns and increasing customer satisfaction.

Blockchain technology, on the other hand, enhances the security and transparency of online transactions. With its decentralized and immutable ledger, blockchain provides a secure platform for transactions, protecting against fraud and ensuring that every transaction is transparent and traceable. This security is especially crucial in an era where data breaches and cyber threats are on the rise. By integrating blockchain, e-commerce platforms can offer a safer shopping experience, fostering trust and loyalty among consumers.

Looking ahead, the future of online shopping appears rich with potential, driven by ongoing innovations in AI and technology. The trend towards more personalized and immersive shopping experiences is likely to accelerate, with AI becoming even more adept at understanding and anticipating consumer needs. Virtual reality (VR) could further enhance the online shopping experience by creating fully immersive virtual stores where you can browse and shop as if you were in a physical store. Additionally, the integration of AI with Internet of Things (IoT) devices could lead to new forms of automated shopping, where your smart refrigerator orders groceries on your behalf based on your consumption patterns and preferences.

As we close this exploration of the evolving landscape of e-commerce, it's clear that the fusion of AI and technology is not just reshaping how we shop; it's fundamentally transforming the relationship between consumers and retailers. By making shopping more personalized, efficient, and secure, these technologies are setting a new standard for consumer expectations and experiences. As we transition into the next chapter, we carry forward the understanding that the future of commerce lies in the seamless integration of technology, data, and innovative thinking, aimed at enriching the consumer journey in every possible way.

Chapter 4:
Preparing for the Digital Future

As the digital age accelerates, the landscape of work and employment continuously evolves, driven by relentless advancements in technology. The specter of automation looms large, a harbinger of change that carries the dual forces of opportunity and disruption. While some view automation as a threat to traditional job sectors, others see it as a catalyst for new realms of employment and innovation. In this chapter, we delve into the strategies and mindsets that can help you future-proof your career against the inevitable shifts brought about by automation. By identifying essential skills, embracing adaptability, and leveraging technology, you can navigate these changes not just with resilience but with a proactive stance that turns potential threats into opportunities for growth and career advancement.

4.1 Future-Proofing Your Career Against Automation

Identify Automation-Resistant Skills

In an era where machines and algorithms increasingly replicate human tasks, certain skills remain distinctly human and, thus, less susceptible to automation. These skills include creative thinking, problem-solving, and interpersonal dynamics. Creative thinking, the ability to imagine new ideas and solutions, is inherently human and difficult for machines to replicate. Problem-solving, especially in complex scenarios involving ethical considerations or ambiguous data, also relies heavily on human intuition and critical thinking. Interpersonal skills, such as empathy, persuasion, and collaboration, are crucial in professions where human interaction is key and are often overlooked in discussions about automation.

As the job market evolves, the workforce must adapt to meet the new demands. This shift necessitates a focus on developing skills in the following areas:

- **Problem-Solving:** Employees need to be adept at identifying issues, analyzing data, and developing effective solutions. This involves both logical reasoning and creative thinking to address novel challenges that automation cannot handle.

- **Critical Thinking:** The ability to evaluate information critically, make decisions based on evidence, and think independently is crucial. Workers must be able to assess situations from multiple perspectives and anticipate the implications of their decisions.

- **Adaptability:** The pace of technological change requires a workforce that is flexible and willing to continuously learn and adapt. Employees must be open to acquiring new skills, embracing new technologies, and shifting roles as needed.

Developing these skills involves a commitment to lifelong learning and personal development. Engaging in diverse experiences, pursuing arts and creativity, participating in team-based activities, and seeking roles that require negotiation and leadership can enhance your repertoire of automation-resistant skills. Additionally, staying informed about industry trends and the impact of automation can help you understand which skills are most valuable and in demand.

Adaptability and Flexibility

Your greatest asset is perhaps your capacity to adapt and remain flexible in a changing job market. Adaptability is not merely about surviving; it's about thriving—transforming challenges into opportunities and disruptions into launchpads for career development. To cultivate adaptability, consider adopting a mindset that embraces change rather than resists it. This might involve reevaluating your career path, continuing education, or pivoting to different roles or industries where the demand is growing.

Strategies for enhancing your adaptability include staying technologically literate, understanding the basics of emerging technologies in your field, and being open to new ways of working, such as remote collaboration or flexible job structures. Networking within your industry and participating in professional forums can also provide insights into how others are adapting to changes, offering blueprints and inspiration for your career.

Leveraging Technology for Career Advancement

Technology is a tool that, when wielded with skill and foresight, can significantly amplify your career prospects. Familiarity with digital tools and platforms that enhance productivity and facilitate new forms of collaboration is crucial. For instance, mastering data analysis tools can provide insights that drive better business decisions, while proficiency in digital communication tools can enhance your ability to work effectively in virtual teams.

Consider also the strategic use of online platforms for personal branding. Platforms such as LinkedIn allow you to network and showcase your professional achievements and thought leadership, increasing your visibility and attractiveness to potential employers or collaborators.

Case Studies of Adaptation

Real-life examples abound of professionals who have successfully navigated the challenges posed by automation. Take, for example, a marketing professional who transitioned from traditional print advertising to digital and social media marketing. Recognizing the shift in industry trends, they embraced learning new digital tools and analytics, eventually leading their company's digital marketing strategy and significantly increasing engagement rates.

Another case is that of a manufacturing worker who, facing job uncertainty due to automation, opted to learn computer-aided design (CAD) and programming. These skills enhanced their role within the company and opened up new opportunities in the design and development sectors, illustrating how traditional roles can evolve and integrate with new technological capabilities.

Each of these cases underscores a fundamental truth: the future belongs to those who are prepared to reinvent themselves, continually learning and adapting to the ever-changing landscape of the digital age. As we move forward, the interplay between human ingenuity and technological advancement will continue to redefine the boundaries of what is possible in the workplace, offering exciting opportunities for those ready to embrace change and make technology work for them.

4.2 The Skills of Tomorrow: What Will Professionals Need?

In an era marked by rapid technological evolution, the demand for a workforce equipped with robust technical skills has never been more critical. Data analytics, coding, and cybersecurity represent the triad of technical competencies that are reshaping the contours of nearly every industry. Data analytics, for instance, has transcended its traditional bastions in finance and marketing to become indispensable in sectors like healthcare, where it helps in predicting patient outcomes, and in urban planning, with its ability to analyze large sets of data for city development. Acquiring skills in data analytics involves a deep dive into statistical methods and tools like Python or R programming, coupled with a persistent knack for interpreting data patterns and anomalies.

Coding, too, is no longer siloed within the tech industry. It has become a fundamental skill that enhances employability across various fields. Understanding programming languages such as Java, Python, or JavaScript can be the gateway to not just software development roles but also to areas like data journalism and digital art, where creating interactive, engaging content is key. Meanwhile, cybersecurity has emerged from the backrooms of IT departments to the forefront of national defense strategies and corporate policies, propelled by the global surge in cyber threats. Cybersecurity skills entail understanding network architectures, encryption protocols, and the latest in penetration testing and ethical hacking techniques.

With manual and repetitive tasks capitulating to AI and automation, a workforce that can master these technical skills is imperative; soft skills—often termed essential skills—are also in high demand in the digital age. Emotional intelligence, the ability to be aware of, control, and express one's emotions and to handle interpersonal relationships judiciously and empathetically, is paramount in an era where AI and machine learning are omnipresent. This skill enhances team interactions and customer relations, fostering a work environment conducive to innovation and productivity. Leadership skills, too, are transforming, tilting towards models that emphasize inclusivity, team empowerment, and a visionary approach to tackling challenges. Moreover, the ability to collaborate effectively across diverse teams and cultures is becoming indispensable as businesses increasingly operate on a global scale. These soft skills can be honed through targeted training programs, mentorship, and real-world experience, emphasizing communication, negotiation, and ethical decision-making. Although there is an emphasis on team dynamics, there is also the need for self-motivated individuals who can work independently and with minimal or no supervision. The ability to leverage the tools and technologies that enable remote work, including collaborative platforms, cloud services, and communication tools, emphasizes their roles in enhancing productivity and connectivity.

The integration of technical prowess with insights from other disciplines—known as cross-disciplinary learning—is another pillar vital for future professionals. In an increasingly complex world, the most innovative solutions often emerge from the intersection of fields. For instance, integrating technology with environmental science can lead to breakthroughs in sustainable energy solutions, while combining programming skills with healthcare can revolutionize telemedicine and patient care. Embracing a cross-disciplinary approach involves both formal education and self-directed learning paths that encourage exploration beyond one's primary field of expertise. This might involve taking courses in both tech fields and liberal arts, participating in workshops that focus on real-world problem-solving, or collaborating on projects that require a blend of skills.

Lifelong learning has become a requisite for maintaining relevance and competitiveness in the workforce. The landscape of work is continuously reshaped by technological advancements, making it essential for professionals to commit to ongoing education. This can be facilitated by engaging with a plethora of available learning resources. Online platforms such as Coursera, edX, and LinkedIn Learning offer courses on everything from blockchain technology to advanced machine learning, often designed in collaboration with leading universities and companies. Workshops, webinars, and professional networks provide avenues for experiential learning and knowledge sharing, crucial for staying updated with the latest industry trends and practices. Moreover, many organizations now support professional development through learning stipends or partnerships with educational institutions, recognizing that investment in employee growth translates directly to organizational success.

Navigating the future will require a delicate balancing act between deepening one's expertise in specific technical areas and broadening knowledge across multiple disciplines. As automation and new technologies continue to transform the workplace, the ability to adapt, learn, and apply diverse skills will define the professional success stories of tomorrow. The commitment to continuous learning, coupled with a strategic approach to skill development, will ensure individual career growth and contribute to the broader goal of driving innovation and progress in an increasingly digital world.

4.3 Cultivating a Continuous Learning Mindset in Tech

In the rapidly evolving sector of technology, adopting a growth mindset is not merely beneficial; it is imperative for those looking to not only survive but thrive in this dynamic environment. A growth mindset, a term popularized by psychologist Carol Dweck, refers to the belief that your abilities and intelligence can be developed over time through dedication and hard work. In the tech industry, where new languages, tools, and predictions emerge at a breakneck pace, the resilience and willingness to learn from failures associated with a growth mindset are invaluable. This mindset encourages you to view challenges as opportunities for growth and to persist in the face of setbacks, a necessary approach when navigating the complex and often unpredictable tech landscape.

Cultivating such a mindset begins with reframing failures as stepping stones to success. In tech, where rapid innovation leads to equally rapid obsolescence, each failure provides critical insights that could lead to breakthroughs in future projects. Embracing this perspective requires a deliberate shift in how you perceive and react to challenges. Instead of feeling defeated by unsuccessful outcomes, analyze them to extract lessons and apply them to future endeavors. This iterative learning process is at the heart of technological advancement and personal growth.

Integrating continuous learning into your daily routine is another crucial strategy for maintaining relevance in the tech field. Setting aside dedicated time for reading industry publications, exploring new technologies, and participating in forums can keep you updated on the latest developments. Experimenting with new tools and techniques, even those outside of your immediate area of expertise, broadens your understanding and enhances your adaptability.

Hackathons, often overlooked, provide a unique opportunity for immersive learning and innovation. These events not only allow you to apply your skills in new and often challenging contexts but also to observe and collaborate with other tech professionals, exposing you to new approaches and workflows.

The role of online platforms in tech education cannot be overstated. Platforms like Coursera, Udemy, and Codecademy offer courses designed by industry experts and are an excellent resource for both beginners and seasoned professionals looking to upgrade their skills. These platforms cover a vast range of topics, from basic programming languages to advanced machine learning algorithms. What sets online learning apart is its flexibility; courses can typically be accessed anytime and from anywhere, allowing you to learn at your own pace and on your schedule. To maximize the benefits of these resources, it is crucial to choose courses that not only align with your career goals but also challenge you to think outside your comfort zone. Engaging actively with course materials, participating in discussion forums, and completing project work are all strategies that enhance the learning experience, making it more comprehensive and practical.

Building a personal learning network is another dimension of developing a growth mindset. This network should include mentors, peers, and industry leaders whose insights and experiences can guide your professional development. Mentors provide guidance, feedback, and support, helping you navigate your career path and learning goals. Peers, on the other hand, can offer different perspectives and collaborations that enrich your understanding and expand your problem-solving capabilities. Finally, staying connected with industry leaders through social media, attending webinars, and participating in industry conferences can provide you with a broader view of the tech landscape, including emerging trends and opportunities. Cultivating these relationships requires consistent engagement and contribution, such as sharing your knowledge and experiences, which reinforces your learning and establishes your reputation in the tech community.

In conclusion, cultivating a continuous learning mindset in tech involves embracing challenges, integrating learning into your daily life, leveraging online resources, and building a supportive network. These strategies ensure not only personal and professional growth but also a meaningful engagement with the ever-evolving world of technology. As you continue to navigate your career in tech, remember that each step in learning is a step towards greater adaptability, innovation, and success.

4.4 Entrepreneurial Opportunities in the Tech Space

Navigating the entrepreneurial landscape in the tech industry demands not only a keen understanding of technology but also an acute sense of market needs and opportunities. For aspiring tech entrepreneurs, the first critical step is identifying gaps in the market where technology can provide innovative solutions. This process involves thorough market research, understanding consumer pain points, and identifying inefficiencies in current technological offerings. Engaging with potential users and industry experts and conducting surveys can provide valuable insights into what is missing or could be improved. For instance, the rise of fintech innovations was largely driven by the traditional banking sector's failure to provide transparent, user-friendly, and accessible services. Entrepreneurs who spotted these gaps were able to create solutions like mobile payment systems and peer-to-peer lending platforms, which revolutionized the financial sector.

Once a market need is identified, the next step is transforming that insight into a viable tech venture. This journey begins with idea validation—confirming that the market need corresponds to a real demand, often through prototypes or pilot programs. Feedback during this phase is crucial, as it helps refine the product to better fit the market's needs. Following validation, securing funding is the next hurdle. Options range from bootstrapping and crowdfunding to angel investors and venture capital, depending on the scale of the venture and the amount of capital needed. The choice of funding also dictates certain dynamics of business growth and investor relations that need careful consideration.

Product development, guided by lean methodology principles, emphasizes iterative development and user feedback to ensure the product effectively meets user needs without overextending resources. It's a process marked by continuous adaptation and refinement, a strategy that significantly mitigates risk. The final step is the market launch, which should be approached with a robust marketing strategy that includes clear messaging and an understanding of the target audience. Digital marketing, especially leveraging social media and content marketing, can be particularly effective in reaching a broad audience at a relatively low cost.

The narrative of tech entrepreneurship is rich with case studies that serve as both instructional guides and inspirational tales. Consider the story of a startup that began with a simple yet compelling idea: a smartphone app that could identify songs playing in the environment around its user. Initial skepticism was rampant—was there a real demand, and how would they monetize it? However, through persistent development, strategic partnerships with music companies, and a clear understanding of their user base, the app became an indispensable tool for music lovers. This success story underscores the importance of clarity of vision and persistence in the face of challenges, elements that are often decisive in differentiating successful ventures from failed startups.

However, the path of entrepreneurship is often fraught with failures and setbacks. A resilient entrepreneur must view each failure as a learning opportunity, a stepping stone in the journey of business creation. When a tech venture encounters obstacles, the ability to pivot—making significant changes to the business model or product based on feedback and new insights—can be crucial. For instance, many successful tech companies today, including major players in the social media and e-commerce sectors, started with different business models but pivoted in response to market feedback and changing conditions. These pivots, though risky, can lead to greater alignment with market needs and, ultimately, greater success.

Handling setbacks also involves maintaining a strong support network and being willing to seek advice and mentorship. The tech industry, with its rapid evolution and complex ecosystems, can be particularly challenging to navigate alone. Engaging with other entrepreneurs, joining industry-specific incubators and accelerators, and participating in networking events can provide crucial support and guidance. Moreover, a clear understanding of the risk involved and having contingency plans can help manage the stress and financial strain that often come with navigating the turbulent waters of tech entrepreneurship.

In this dynamic environment, the tech entrepreneur must be a versatile innovator, a keen observer of market trends, and, most importantly, resilient in the face of inevitable challenges and setbacks. The journey of creating and sustaining a tech venture is as challenging as it is rewarding, offering an unparalleled opportunity to transform innovative ideas into tangible solutions that can reshape industries. As technology continues to advance, the potential for impactful entrepreneurship expands, inviting bold visionaries to step forward and shape the future of technology and commerce.

4.5 Investing in Technology: Trends and Practical Tips

In the dynamic realm of technology, where innovation emerges as both a disruptor and a catalyst, investing can seem like navigating a labyrinthine galaxy of opportunities and risks. The allure of potentially high returns from sectors such as artificial intelligence (AI), blockchain, and sustainable technology is compelling. AI, for instance, is not just transforming existing industries but also creating new markets altogether. From healthcare applications that predict patient diseases to AI-driven automation in manufacturing, the expansion is robust and multifaceted. Similarly, blockchain technology extends far beyond its initial association with cryptocurrencies. Today, it's pioneering changes in supply chain transparency and secure digital transactions, presenting unique investment opportunities. Moreover, as the global dialogue shifts towards sustainability, technology aimed at promoting energy efficiency and reducing environmental footprints is also seeing increased investment interest. These technologies promise not only profitability but also longevity as they align with broader economic and social trends steering toward automation, digitization, and sustainability.

However, investing in such rapidly evolving sectors requires a keen understanding of the inherent risks, including market volatility and technological obsolescence. Market volatility in tech sectors is fueled by several factors, including regulatory changes, market entry of groundbreaking products, or even shifts in consumer behavior driven by technological advancements. Technological obsolescence, on the other hand, poses a unique challenge as today's pioneering technology can quickly become tomorrow's history due to the rapid pace of innovation in the tech industry. To navigate these waters, conducting thorough due diligence is crucial. This includes analyzing company fundamentals, understanding the specific technologies, and staying updated with industry trends and regulatory landscapes. Additionally, potential investors should consider the scalability of the technology, the expertise of the company's leadership, and the competitive landscape within the sector.

Diversifying investments within the tech sector is another strategic approach to mitigate risks and enhance potential returns. Just as a well-balanced diet varies protein, fruits, and carbohydrates, a well-balanced investment portfolio spreads capital across different technologies and companies of varying maturity levels. For instance, while one might invest in a well-established AI analytics company, balancing that with investments in emerging blockchain startups or renewable energy technologies can mitigate risk. This strategy not only cushions against fluctuations in one area but also positions you to benefit from growth across the broader tech spectrum. Effective diversification requires understanding the different sub-sectors within the tech industry and their respective growth potentials and risk factors.

Moreover, the decision between long-term versus short-term investments in technology can significantly impact your investment outcomes. Long-term investments often align well with technology sectors, where growth trajectories are strong but gradual. For instance, investing in sustainable tech like solar energy technologies or electric vehicles can be fruitful eventually as global energy policies shift towards sustainability. These investments might require patience, but as infrastructures adapt and technologies mature, the potential for substantial returns grows. On the contrary, short-term investments can be advantageous in areas experiencing rapid innovation cycles, such as mobile technologies or software development, where products and services can quickly gain market adoption and generate swift returns. However, they typically require a higher tolerance for risk and a proactive approach to managing the investment portfolio, ready to make quick decisions based on market trends and technological advancements.

Navigating the investment landscape in technology demands a blend of enthusiasm for innovation with a disciplined approach to risk management. It requires an ongoing commitment to education and adaptation, leveraging detailed research and diversified strategies to capitalize on the opportunities of today while mitigating the uncertainties of tomorrow. As you delve into this exciting yet complex field, remember that the convergence of technology and investment is not just about financial returns but also about participating in the advancements that shape our future.

4.6 The Global Impact of Digital Transformation on Businesses

In the rapidly evolving business landscape, digital transformation emerges as a pivotal force, revolutionizing operations through innovative integration of technologies like automation, data analytics, and customer relationship management (CRM). These digital tools streamline operations, enhance efficiency, and create new value propositions in a competitive market. Automation, for instance, reduces the need for repetitive tasks, allowing human resources to focus on more strategic activities that require human insight. Data analytics, on the other hand, equips businesses with the ability to make informed decisions based on real-time data, offering insights into customer behaviors, market trends, and operational efficiencies. This analytical capacity enables businesses to tailor their services to better meet customer expectations and spot market opportunities swiftly.

Digital technologies have transformed CRM systems, evolving into robust platforms that facilitate not just customer management but also predictive analytics and comprehensive customer engagement strategies. These systems help businesses anticipate customer needs and foster personalized interactions, thus enhancing customer satisfaction and loyalty. For example, advanced CRM systems can analyze customer feedback and interaction patterns to predict future buying behaviors and tailor marketing strategies accordingly. This strategic approach optimizes marketing efforts and enhances customer engagement and retention, critical factors in today's customer-centric business environment.

Digital transformation also plays a crucial role in driving international collaboration. Technology enables businesses to operate and collaborate across borders more effectively than ever before. Cloud computing, for instance, allows team members in different parts of the world to access the same information and work on projects simultaneously, regardless of location. This real-time collaboration is vital for global businesses that rely on coordination across various time zones and geographies. Moreover, digital communication tools such as video conferencing and real-time messaging have made it easier and more efficient for teams to stay connected and productive, regardless of physical distance.

For small and medium enterprises (SMEs), digital transformation presents both significant opportunities and notable challenges. On the positive side, technologies like e-commerce platforms and digital marketing tools can level the playing field, allowing SMEs to reach wider markets and compete with larger players. Digital tools provide SMEs with cost-effective solutions for operations, marketing, and customer service, enabling them to enhance their competitiveness and growth potential. However, the challenges include limited resources for implementing advanced technologies and a lack of digital literacy, which can hinder the ability to fully leverage the benefits of digital transformation. Overcoming these challenges often requires strategic planning and sometimes partnership or external support to navigate the digital landscape effectively.

Case Studies of Transformation

The transformative impact of digital technologies can be illustrated through various case studies that highlight both the strategies used and the outcomes achieved. Consider a traditional retail company that transitioned to an omnichannel approach by integrating e-commerce with its physical stores. By leveraging digital tools to track inventory and customer preferences, the company was able to offer a seamless shopping experience, whether the customer shopped online or in-store. This integration improved customer satisfaction and increased sales and operational efficiency.

Another example involves a manufacturing SME that implemented IoT (Internet of Things) technologies to monitor equipment and predict maintenance needs. This proactive approach prevented unexpected downtime, enhanced the equipment's lifespan, and optimized the production process. The digital transformation, in this case, improved operational efficiency and resulted in substantial cost savings and increased production capacity.

These case studies exemplify how businesses, from retail to manufacturing, can effectively utilize digital technologies to transform their operations, enhance customer experiences, and improve their competitive edge in the market. The key to successful digital transformation lies in understanding the specific needs of the business and integrating technologies that address those needs effectively.

As the digital landscape continues to evolve, the impact of digital transformation on businesses around the globe will undoubtedly continue to grow. This ongoing evolution presents businesses with both challenges and opportunities, requiring continuous adaptation and innovation. The ability to effectively integrate digital technologies into business operations is becoming a critical factor in achieving sustainable growth and success in the modern economy. As we conclude this exploration of digital transformation, it is clear that the integration of technology in business is not just about automation or efficiency—it is about fundamentally rethinking how businesses operate and deliver value in an increasingly digital world. This chapter sets the stage for the next, where we will explore the broader implications of digital transformation on global economic patterns and societal changes.

Chapter 5:
Addressing Tech-Driven Global Challenges

As we navigate the complexities of our evolving planet, the dual forces of technology and environmental concern have become increasingly intertwined. The burgeoning impact of climate change commands not just attention but action—sophisticated, coordinated, and technology-driven action. This chapter delves into how modern technology, particularly advanced computing, artificial intelligence (AI), and the Internet of Things (IoT), stands not only as a witness to environmental degradation but also as a potent tool in our fight against it. From the intricate modeling of climate patterns to the development of carbon capture technologies and the optimization of energy use through smart grids, technology's role in environmental stewardship is both powerful and promising.

5.1 Technology in the Fight Against Climate Change

Climate Modeling and Data Analysis

The task of predicting weather patterns and assessing the impacts of climate change has grown increasingly complex and urgent. In this intricate endeavor, advanced computing and AI emerge as pivotal allies. By harnessing vast computing power, climate scientists can simulate and analyze countless scenarios under different climate models, leading to predictions that are not only more accurate but also highly detailed across geographic and temporal scales. These simulations allow for the visualization of long-term climate trends and immediate weather events, providing crucial data that informs both policy decisions and public awareness.

AI, in its capacity to handle large datasets efficiently, further refines these predictive models. Through machine learning algorithms, AI systems can identify patterns and anomalies in historical climate data, learning iteratively to improve the accuracy of their predictions. This capability is vital for understanding potential future states of the Earth's climate system under various carbon emission scenarios, thereby informing strategies for mitigation and adaptation. For instance, AI-driven models have been used to predict sea-level rise, giving coastal communities valuable information for planning and resilience building.

Carbon Capture and Storage Technologies

As the global community grapples with reducing greenhouse gas emissions, carbon capture and storage (CCS) technologies present a critical solution. These technologies involve capturing carbon dioxide (CO_2) emissions at their source—such as power plants and industrial processes—transporting them to a storage site, and depositing them underground in rock formations where they won't enter the atmosphere. Recent advancements in this field have improved the efficiency and feasibility of CCS, making it a more viable option for large-scale deployment.

Innovations in materials science, for example, have led to the development of better absorbents that can capture CO_2 more effectively and at lower costs. Additionally, AI has found a role in optimizing the processes of capture, transport, and storage, reducing energy consumption, and increasing safety. By integrating sensor data and predictive analytics, AI systems can monitor and adjust operational parameters in real-time, ensuring that the CCS process is both efficient and secure.

Smart Grids and Energy Efficiency

The transformation of our energy systems is another frontier where technology plays a crucial role. Smart grids, enhanced by IoT devices, represent a significant leap in how energy is distributed and managed. These grids use digital communication technology to detect and react to local changes in electricity usage, improving the efficiency of electricity distribution. IoT devices contribute to this ecosystem by providing real-time data on energy consumption from various sources, including residential, commercial, and industrial sectors.

This data enables more informed decision-making regarding energy production and distribution, leading to reduced energy wastage and enhanced grid reliability. For instance, during times of low demand, smart grids can adjust to decrease production, thus conserving energy and reducing operational costs. Conversely, during peak periods, they can manage the load by rerouting power or temporarily reducing supply to non-essential areas, thereby preventing outages and promoting energy conservation.

Public Awareness and Engagement Tools

In the digital age, technology significantly bolsters public engagement and awareness. Various platforms and applications have been developed to actively engage you in climate action. Carbon footprint calculators, for example, allow individuals to understand and manage their personal impact on the environment by estimating the amount of carbon dioxide generated by their activities and suggesting ways to reduce it. Real-time pollution tracking apps provide users with data about air quality in their immediate environment, enabling more informed decisions about outdoor activities and health precautions.

These tools empower individual action and foster a broader cultural shift towards environmental responsibility. By making environmental data accessible and understandable, technology demystifies abstract concepts like carbon footprints, making the effects of climate change more tangible and immediate. This transparency is crucial in building sustained public engagement and driving collective action towards a more sustainable future.

In harnessing the power of technology to address the global challenge of climate change, we are reminded of our responsibility to act and innovate responsibly. As we continue to explore the capabilities of advanced technologies in environmental conservation, the path forward requires a careful balance between technological advancement and sustainable practices. The integration of technology in our environmental strategies, while offering profound benefits, also demands continuous evaluation and adaptation to ensure that our technological solutions do not inadvertently contribute to the very problems they aim to solve.

5.2 Innovations in Renewable Energy Technologies

Advancements in Solar Power

The relentless pursuit of enhancing solar power technology has yielded innovations that push the boundaries of efficiency and reduce costs, making solar energy more accessible and sustainable. Perovskite solar cells, for instance, represent a significant breakthrough in this arena. Unlike traditional silicon-based solar cells, perovskite cells are made from a hybrid organic-inorganic lead or tin halide-based material that offers excellent light absorption and charge-carrier mobilities. This technology has achieved superior efficiencies in converting sunlight to electricity at a lower cost, thanks to the cheaper materials and simpler manufacturing processes involved. Moreover, the flexibility of perovskite cells allows for their integration into various surfaces, paving the way for their use in everything from building windows to personal devices, transforming everyday surfaces into energy-generating entities.

Another innovative development in solar technology is the emergence of solar skins. These photovoltaic materials are designed to mimic the appearance of roof tiles and other building materials, allowing solar panels to blend seamlessly into the architecture of a building without compromising aesthetic values. This advancement not only enhances the visual appeal of solar panels but also increases their adoption in residential areas, where homeowners might be concerned about the aesthetic impact of traditional solar installations. By integrating these solar skins, buildings can maintain their traditional appearance while contributing to energy sustainability, a dual benefit that accelerates the adoption of solar technology in urban landscapes.

Wind Energy Innovations

In the realm of wind energy, significant advancements have been made to increase the efficiency and viability of harnessing wind power. Offshore wind farms, for example, have gained traction due to their ability to capture the stronger and more consistent winds available at sea compared to those on land. These installations, while more complex and costly due to their maritime location, can generate more power and thus offer a higher return on investment over time. The strategic placement of these turbines, often in deeper waters, leverages advanced foundation designs and floating technologies that were not previously available, pushing the boundaries of where and how wind energy can be harvested.

Another noteworthy innovation in this sector is the development of vertical-axis wind turbines (VAWTs). Unlike their horizontal-axis counterparts, VAWTs are omnidirectional, meaning they can harness wind from any direction. This ability eliminates the need for orientation mechanisms, simplifying the design and reducing maintenance costs. VAWTs are particularly suitable for urban environments where wind directions can be highly variable. The compact and versatile design of these turbines allows them to be installed on rooftops and in other confined spaces, making them an excellent solution for decentralized energy production in densely populated areas.

Geothermal and Hydropower

Geothermal energy extraction has also seen remarkable improvements, particularly with the development of enhanced geothermal systems (EGS). Traditional geothermal power relies on natural reservoirs of hot water, but EGS can create reservoirs in areas where hot rock is available but water is scarce. By injecting water into these rocks, EGS technologies facilitate the extraction of heat from the earth, significantly expanding the potential for geothermal energy beyond natural reservoir locations. This method not only increases the geographic diversity of geothermal energy production but also enhances its reliability and sustainability as a power source.

In the sphere of hydroelectric power, advancements have focused on increasing the efficiency and environmental compatibility of hydro installations. Small-scale hydro generators, which can be installed in small rivers or streams without the need for large dams, minimize the ecological impact traditionally associated with hydroelectric power. These systems are particularly beneficial for rural communities, providing a reliable and renewable energy source without the extensive infrastructure and ecological disruption caused by larger-scale installations.

Integration Challenges and Solutions

Despite these innovations, integrating renewable energy sources into existing power grids presents significant challenges. The intermittent nature of sources like solar and wind requires advanced solutions to ensure a stable energy supply. Energy storage systems, such as batteries and other forms of energy storage, play a crucial role in mitigating this intermittency by storing excess energy generated during peak production times and releasing it during demand peaks or low production periods.

Also, grid modernization is essential to accommodate the increasing share of renewable energy. Smart grids, which use digital technology to monitor and manage the transport of electricity from all generation sources to meet the varying electricity demands of end-users, are crucial in this aspect. These grids can dynamically adjust flows to integrate intermittent renewable energies smoothly, ensuring that the transition towards a more sustainable energy grid minimizes disruptions and maintains reliability. The implementation of these technologies, while challenging, is essential for the creation of a resilient, efficient, and sustainable energy infrastructure that can handle the complexities of renewable energy integration, paving the way for a cleaner, greener future.

5.3 Tech Solutions for Global Health Crises

In the vast expanse of global health, where challenges such as access to care and epidemic response are intensified by geographical and economic disparities, technology emerges as a crucial ally. Telemedicine and remote diagnostics, for example, have revolutionized the way healthcare is delivered, particularly in underserved regions. These technological interventions allow medical practitioners to extend their reach far beyond the confines of traditional medical facilities, providing essential health services to remote and rural communities where healthcare would otherwise be inaccessible. Through platforms that support video conferencing, healthcare professionals can conduct virtual consultations, enabling them to diagnose and manage patients without the need for physical travel. This maximizes the efficiency of healthcare delivery and significantly reduces the costs associated with accessing medical care, making it more affordable and accessible to a broader population.

The impact of telemedicine became particularly pronounced during global health emergencies, such as the COVID-19 pandemic. As healthcare systems around the world were stretched to their limits, telemedicine offered a viable alternative to in-person visits, helping to alleviate the burden on healthcare facilities while reducing the risk of virus transmission. Remote diagnostics played a pivotal role during this period, with technologies such as digital stethoscopes and mobile health apps enabling the monitoring of patients' conditions remotely. These tools not only facilitated the timely detection and treatment of the disease but also ensured the continuity of care for non-COVID-related conditions, maintaining the overall health of the population during the crisis.

AI in Epidemic Prediction and Response

Artificial intelligence has carved a niche for itself at the forefront of epidemic prediction and response. By integrating diverse data sources, including historical epidemiological data, real-time health reports, and demographic information, AI models can predict the outbreak and spread of infectious diseases with remarkable accuracy. These predictions are crucial for early warning systems, enabling governments and health organizations to implement preventive measures and allocate resources more effectively.

Recent global health crises have underscored the value of AI in managing public health responses. For instance, during the Ebola outbreak in West Africa, AI was used to predict the spread of the virus, informing containment strategies that were critical in limiting the outbreak. Similarly, AI-driven analytics were employed during the COVID-19 pandemic to model disease transmission patterns and assess the impact of various intervention strategies, such as social distancing and lockdown measures. These tools provided policymakers with the evidence needed to make informed decisions during a rapidly evolving situation, showcasing the potential of AI to support complex public health strategies.

Wearable Health Monitors in Disease Prevention

Wearable technologies have transcended their initial consumer-focused applications to play a significant role in disease prevention and health monitoring. Wearable health monitors, equipped with sensors to track vital signs such as heart rate, blood pressure, and oxygen saturation provide continuous health data that can be critical for early disease detection and management. By analyzing trends in this data, healthcare providers can identify potential health issues before they become severe, enabling proactive management of conditions such as heart disease and diabetes.

In addition, wearables have the potential to support personalized medicine approaches by providing data that is specific to the individual's health status, lifestyle, and environmental conditions. This data, when analyzed over time, can offer unique insights into the factors that influence an individual's health, leading to customized health plans that optimize disease prevention and management. The integration of wearables into routine health care not only empowers individuals to take charge of their health but also enhances the ability of healthcare systems to provide timely and effective interventions.

Vaccine Development and Distribution Technologies

The rapid development and distribution of vaccines are critical in the fight against infectious diseases, particularly in low-resource settings where the burden of disease is often greatest. Recent advancements in technology have significantly accelerated vaccine development, with platforms like mRNA technology enabling scientists to design vaccines in a fraction of the time traditionally required. These platforms allow for the rapid synthesis of vaccines by using a genetic code that instructs cells to produce vaccine proteins, a method that proved pivotal in the swift development of COVID-19 vaccines.

In addition to accelerating vaccine development, technology also plays a crucial role in improving distribution logistics. Cold chain technologies, which ensure that vaccines are stored and transported at the required temperatures, have become more sophisticated, incorporating IoT sensors and real-time data tracking to monitor the conditions of vaccine shipments. This technology ensures the integrity of vaccines during distribution, particularly in regions where infrastructure may be lacking.

Moreover, digital health passports and blockchain technology are being explored for managing vaccine records and distribution. These technological solutions provide secure and verifiable records of vaccinations that are accessible to health providers and patients alike. They streamline the distribution process and enhance the transparency and efficiency of vaccine deployment, ensuring that vaccines reach those in need quickly and reliably.

As we continue to harness these technologies, the horizon of possibilities in global health expands, bringing us closer to a world where healthcare is more accessible, responsive, and efficient. While complex, the integration of technology in healthcare strategies offers a pathway to overcoming some of the most persistent challenges in global health, paving the way for more resilient health systems and healthier populations worldwide.

5.4 Digital Tools for Disaster Response and Management

In the face of natural disasters, the rapid and effective gathering and analysis of data are paramount to saving lives and mitigating damage. Modern technologies, specifically drones, satellites, and Internet of Things (IoT) devices, play an indispensable role in enhancing disaster response efforts through real-time data collection and analysis. Drones, equipped with high-resolution cameras and sensors, can be deployed quickly to disaster zones, where they provide critical information by capturing images and videos from areas that are too dangerous or inaccessible for human responders.

These aerial views offer immediate insights into the extent of damage, help in locating survivors, and assist in assessing the structural integrity of buildings and roads. The agility and perspective offered by drones speed up the response and enhance the safety of rescue teams by highlighting potential hazards.

Satellites, on a broader scale, contribute to disaster management by monitoring weather patterns and tracking the development of severe events such as hurricanes or floods. The data collected by satellites, which include weather forecasts, storm trajectories, and precipitation maps, are crucial for early warning systems. This satellite information, when analyzed alongside historical data, helps predict disaster impacts, allowing authorities to make informed evacuation decisions and prepare resources accordingly. Moreover, satellites provide uninterrupted communication links, a critical component in maintaining coordination among various disaster response agencies when terrestrial communication systems are compromised.

IoT devices further augment disaster response by creating networks of connected sensors that monitor environmental changes in real time. These sensors can detect shifts in parameters such as temperature, moisture levels, and air quality, which are indicative of potential hazards like forest fires or chemical leaks. The interconnected nature of IoT devices means that information can be shared instantaneously across platforms, ensuring that both responders and the public receive timely updates. This network of sensors not only aids in immediate disaster response but also in long-term monitoring and preparedness, adapting and sending alerts based on predictive analytics derived from accumulated data.

Mobile Applications for Disaster Preparedness and Response

In today's digital age, mobile applications have become vital tools in disaster preparedness and response, providing functionalities that range from sending alerts to facilitating communication. Apps designed for disaster response often include features such as real-time alerts, safety information, and user-friendly interfaces that allow individuals to report their status and locate emergency services. For example, apps that integrate geolocation can send targeted alerts to users based on their proximity to affected areas, ensuring that warnings are both timely and relevant. Additionally, these apps often provide step-by-step guides on how to respond to various types of disasters, from natural events like earthquakes to man-made incidents such as industrial accidents, empowering individuals with the knowledge to protect themselves and their families.

What is more, some mobile applications are designed to function even when traditional communication infrastructures fail. These apps use mesh networking technologies that allow smartphones to connect directly with each other via Bluetooth or Wi-Fi, creating a network through which information can be shared. This feature is particularly useful in scenarios where cellular networks are down, ensuring that communication among community members and with emergency responders remains possible. By leveraging the ubiquity of smartphones, these apps play a crucial role in enhancing community resilience and providing a decentralized platform for information dissemination and coordination during emergencies.

Virtual Reality Training for Emergency Responders

Virtual reality (VR) technology has transcended its origins in entertainment to become a transformative tool in training emergency responders. Through realistic, immersive simulations, VR prepares them for an assortment of disaster scenarios that would be impossible or impractical to recreate physically. These virtual environments can simulate complex and dangerous conditions, allowing responders to experience and respond to high-risk situations in a controlled and safe setting. For instance, VR can recreate the chaotic environment of a post-earthquake urban landscape, complete with unstable buildings and scattered debris. Trainees can navigate these scenarios to practice search and rescue operations, medical response, and disaster assessment without the actual physical dangers.

The realism provided by VR extends to sensory experiences—visual, auditory, and sometimes even tactile feedback—that enhance the learning process. This multisensory engagement ensures that responders are not only intellectually prepared but are also emotionally and psychologically conditioned to handle the stress and unpredictability of real-life disasters. Furthermore, VR training can be easily modified to include new data, emerging threats, or updated techniques, allowing training programs to adapt swiftly to the evolving nature of disaster response. By providing this dynamic and adaptable training tool, VR significantly contributes to the preparedness and effectiveness of emergency teams, ultimately improving their performance and the safety of both the responders and the civilians they assist.

Post-Disaster Recovery and Reconstruction

Following the immediate response to a disaster, the focus shifts to recovery and reconstruction, phases that are critical in restoring normalcy and rebuilding affected communities. Digital tools play an essential role in coordinating these efforts, facilitating the efficient allocation of resources and the rebuilding of infrastructure. Project management software, for example, allows for the detailed planning and tracking of recovery projects, from debris removal to the reconstruction of homes and public facilities. These tools enable disaster recovery teams to prioritize tasks, allocate resources optimally, and monitor progress in real-time, ensuring that recovery efforts are both effective and transparent.

Geographic Information Systems (GIS) are particularly valuable in the reconstruction phase. By providing detailed maps and spatial analyses of affected areas, GIS tools help planners and engineers design recovery efforts that are sensitive to the local geography and community needs. For instance, GIS can be used to identify the most impacted areas, plan the locations of temporary housing, or assess the environmental impact of reconstruction activities. This spatial analysis is crucial for making informed decisions that promote sustainable recovery and reduce the vulnerability of rebuilt areas to future disasters.

In addition to these project-focused tools, digital platforms that facilitate community involvement in the recovery process are increasingly important. Online platforms can engage residents in recovery planning, ensuring that their needs and insights are considered. These platforms can also serve as valuable communication tools, providing updates on recovery progress, disseminating safety information, and maintaining a dialogue between recovery teams and the community. By involving the community and ensuring transparency through digital tools, the post-discovery recovery process rebuilds structures and restores trust and resilience within the community.

As we explore the multifaceted role of technology in disaster management, from the initial response to long-term recovery, it becomes clear that our ability to leverage digital tools can significantly enhance our resilience to disasters. These technologies, by providing critical information, facilitating effective communication, and ensuring efficient resource management, empower both responders and communities, shaping a more prepared and resilient society in the face of natural disasters.

5.5 Addressing the Digital Divide: Access to Technology

In an era where digital connectivity is nearly as essential as the utilities that power our homes, the digital divide remains a significant barrier. This divide not only separates the technologically privileged from the underserved but also highlights a gap that can stifle economic opportunities and social mobility. Addressing this requires not only innovative technological solutions but also a concerted effort to ensure these solutions reach the most remote and impoverished areas. Initiatives dedicated to expanding global internet access, such as those employing satellite internet services and solar-powered Wi-Fi stations, have begun to change the landscape of connectivity. These initiatives are crucial in remote areas where traditional broadband infrastructure is either too costly or physically impractical to deploy.

Satellite internet services, for instance, provide connectivity through a network of orbiting satellites that cover a much larger area than terrestrial base stations, making them ideal for rural and remote regions. This technology allows individuals in these areas to access vital online resources, participate in the digital economy, and connect with the broader global community, thus bridging a significant part of the digital divide. Similarly, solar-powered Wi-Fi stations offer a sustainable and cost-effective solution for internet access in regions without reliable electricity. By harnessing solar energy, these stations can operate autonomously, providing uninterrupted internet service to communities that might otherwise remain disconnected. The impact of these technologies extends beyond mere connectivity; they empower communities through access to educational resources, healthcare information, and economic opportunities, fundamentally altering the trajectory of development in these areas.

The issue of affordability also plays a pivotal role in technology access. Efforts to produce affordable computing devices, such as low-cost laptops and tablets, are essential in making digital tools accessible to a broader audience. Organizations and companies around the globe have initiated programs to design and distribute devices that offer basic functionalities at reduced prices without compromising on the quality necessary for educational and professional tasks. These devices often come with pre-installed educational software or subsidized data plans, making them a gateway for underserved populations to leapfrog into the digital age. By lowering the cost barrier, these initiatives democratize access to technology and stimulate local innovations and entrepreneurship, creating a ripple effect that can uplift entire communities.

Educational programs and partnerships play a critical role in transforming access into ability. Across the globe, numerous initiatives focus on enhancing digital literacy, particularly in developing countries where the lack of such skills can be a significant obstacle. Partnerships between governments, non-profit organizations, and tech companies have launched extensive programs aimed at training teachers, providing digital resources to schools, and creating community learning centers that offer free or low-cost access to the internet and learning materials. These educational programs are tailored to meet the specific needs of the communities they serve, addressing not only how to use technology but also how to apply it effectively in everyday life and work environments.

Despite these efforts, the digital divide persists, presenting ongoing challenges that require innovative solutions and inclusive strategies. One of the primary challenges is ensuring that access to technology is not only widespread but also equitable. This means addressing disparities that exist not just between urban and rural areas but also among different demographic groups within those areas. Strategies to enhance inclusivity involve understanding the unique needs and circumstances of these populations, which may include language barriers, cultural differences, and varying levels of literacy and education. Tailoring programs to these needs while also ensuring that marginalized groups have a voice in how these technologies are implemented is crucial for the success of any digital inclusion strategy.

As we continue to push the boundaries of what's possible in technology, our responsibility extends beyond innovation to ensure that these advancements are accessible to all. This commitment to inclusivity not only bridges the digital divide but also harnesses the full potential of technology as a force for good, paving the way for a more connected and empowered global community.

5.6 Technology and Human Rights: Tools for Advocacy and Protection

The digital landscape offers potent tools for monitoring and advocating for human rights, yet it also presents complex challenges that can undermine these very freedoms. Digital platforms and social media have transformed into powerful mechanisms for monitoring human rights abuses. Activists and organizations use these tools to document unlawful incidents and mobilize global responses swiftly. By leveraging platforms like Twitter and Facebook, human rights groups can broadcast real-time information from remote or restricted areas, bypassing traditional media channels that may be censored or slow to react. This immediate global visibility pressures governments and institutions to adhere to human rights standards and provides crucial evidence for legal proceedings aimed at justice and reparation.

However, the power of digital platforms extends beyond dissemination. Sophisticated software tools analyze vast amounts of data to detect patterns that might indicate human rights violations. For instance, algorithms designed to sift through online content can identify changes in sentiment or the emergence of specific terms that correlate with emerging crises. This capability allows human rights organizations to react more proactively rather than solely in response to violations, potentially preventing escalation and saving lives.

Encryption and secure communication tools form the backbone of modern digital security, particularly for activists and vulnerable populations. In regions where surveillance and repression are prevalent, encrypted messaging apps like Signal provide a lifeline for safe communication. Encryption scrambles data so that it can only be accessed by the intended recipient with a decryption key, protecting the privacy and safety of individuals who might otherwise be targeted for their activities. Similarly, Virtual Private Networks (VPNs) obscure users' digital footprints, allowing them to bypass internet censorship and access restricted information without fear of reprisal. These tools are not just technical solutions; they are essential components of modern advocacy, enabling activists to coordinate, mobilize, and advocate without compromising their security.

The role of AI in human rights advocacy is becoming increasingly significant as organizations harness its potential to analyze large datasets quickly and identify patterns of abuse. AI can process information from various sources, including satellite imagery, social media, and news reports, to detect signs of human rights violations, such as mass movements of people, destruction of property, and the emergence of conflict zones. This analysis can provide early warnings of potential crises, allowing for timely intervention. Furthermore, AI-driven facial recognition technology can be used to identify victims and perpetrators of human rights abuses, adding a layer of accountability that was previously unattainable.

Despite these advancements, the dual-use nature of technology poses significant risks. The same tools used to protect human rights can also be employed to violate them. For instance, governments can use surveillance technology to track and repress activists, while facial recognition systems can be misused to target specific ethnic or political groups. The challenge lies in ensuring these technologies are used ethically and that there are stringent safeguards against misuse.

Mitigating these risks requires a multifaceted approach. Legal frameworks must be established to govern the use of surveillance and AI technologies, ensuring they respect privacy and human rights.

Transparency in the deployment of these technologies is crucial; the public should be informed about how and why they are used, and there should be avenues for recourse if abuses occur. Additionally, the development of technology can be guided by ethical principles, ensuring that human rights are considered at every stage of the design and deployment process.

In exploring the intricate relationship between technology and human rights, we uncover a landscape filled with both promise and peril. As we harness these digital tools to protect and promote human rights, we must remain vigilant against their potential to infringe upon those same rights. The path forward is one of responsible innovation, guided by a commitment to upholding the dignity and rights of all individuals.

Chapter 6:
The Future of Work and Society

As the digital tide reshapes the shores of our professional landscapes, we find ourselves navigating the profound transformations ushered in by the remote work revolution. The very fabric of what constitutes a workplace is being redefined as traditional office environments give way to digital spaces that can be accessed from virtually anywhere. This shift, catalyzed by advancements in technology, not only reconfigures the physical boundaries of work but also fundamentally alters the dynamics of productivity, corporate culture, and future employment practices. As we explore these changes, it becomes evident that the technologies enabling remote work are not merely tools but catalysts for a broader evolution in the way society perceives and engages with work.

6.1 The Remote Work Revolution: Technologies Leading the Change

Enabling Technologies

At the heart of the remote work revolution lie several key technologies that have transformed the feasibility and efficiency of working outside traditional office settings. Cloud computing stands as a pillar in this new environment, offering scalable, on-demand access to computing resources without direct active management by users. This technology allows you to access your work-related files and applications from any device, anywhere, seamlessly integrating your work life into your personal space without the need for physical storage or powerful hardware.

Collaboration tools have also been pivotal. Platforms like Slack, Microsoft Teams, and Zoom have become household names, providing robust solutions for communication and collaboration. These tools support a range of functionalities, from video conferencing and instant messaging to project management and file sharing, effectively bridging the gap between dispersed teams. Secure remote access technologies, including VPNs and encrypted connections, ensure that the integrity and confidentiality of communications are maintained, safeguarding company data across the less secure networks typically found in home environments.

Impact on Productivity

The impact of remote work on productivity has been a topic of much debate and study. Initial concerns that remote work might lead to a drop in employee productivity have been largely contradicted by recent research. Studies indicate that the absence of a daily commute, fewer office interruptions, and a customizable work environment can actually enhance an employee's focus and efficiency. However, these benefits are not universal; the productivity gains depend significantly on the nature of the job, the individual's home environment, and the quality of the tools available to them. Challenges such as digital fatigue, the blurring of work-life boundaries, and the need for self-motivation can offset these advantages. It is crucial, therefore, for organizations to provide support and structure that help employees navigate these challenges.

Corporate Culture and Remote Work

Remote work is reshaping corporate culture by decoupling work from a specific location and, in doing so, fostering a culture that values output over presence. This shift has significant implications for how team dynamics and employee relationships are managed. Virtual teams must find new ways to foster trust and cohesion without the benefit of physical proximity. Leaders are now tasked with cultivating a shared sense of purpose and belonging through digital channels, a challenge that requires both innovative thinking and a recommitment to corporate values. Furthermore, remote work can democratize participation in meetings and decision-making processes, as digital platforms often provide more employees with a 'seat at the table,' potentially leading to more inclusive and diverse workplace cultures.

Future Trends

Looking ahead, the trajectory of remote work technologies appears poised for continued innovation and expansion. Virtual reality (VR) and augmented reality (AR) are on the cusp of transforming remote interactions, offering more immersive and interactive meeting experiences that could replicate the nuances of in-person communications. Imagine donning a VR headset to enter a digital workspace where you can collaborate with colleagues from around the globe as if you were in the same room. Meanwhile, AI-driven project management tools are becoming increasingly sophisticated, capable of automating routine tasks, optimizing workflows, and even predicting project risks before they arise. These technologies promise not only to enhance the efficiency of remote work but also to redefine the very essence of what it means to be "at work."

As we continue to navigate the complexities of this new era, the technologies that facilitate remote work will undoubtedly play a pivotal role in shaping the future of our societies and economies. They offer a glimpse into a world where work is not a place you go to but a thing you do — anytime, anywhere. This paradigm shift challenges old norms and opens up new possibilities for how, when, and where work can be done, heralding a future that values flexibility, autonomy, and the seamless integration of work and life. As these trends unfold, they invite us to rethink not only our work practices but also our societal structures, preparing us for a future that promises both unprecedented freedom and novel challenges.

6.2 The Societal Impact of Near-Universal Automation

Economic Effects

The advent of automation is reshaping the economic landscape at an unprecedented pace, introducing complexities that straddle both boon and bane. Economically, widespread automation is poised to increase productivity and efficiency, reducing costs for businesses and potentially leading to lower prices for consumers. However, the displacement of jobs through automated technologies presents a significant challenge, particularly in sectors such as manufacturing, transportation, and retail, where routine tasks are more susceptible to automation. This shift threatens to exacerbate income inequality, as the economic benefits of automation often accumulate to those who possess the capital and skills to leverage new technologies, leaving behind a substantial portion of the workforce.

The polarization of job opportunities—where high-skill jobs that require complex problem-solving abilities and low-skill jobs that necessitate personal interactions are less likely to be automated—further intensifies economic disparities. Middle-skill jobs, which have traditionally provided a stable income for middle-class families, are declining, contributing to economic bifurcation. This economic restructuring necessitates a reevaluation of income distribution mechanisms and may even call for radical approaches to ensure financial stability for those displaced by machines.

Social Changes

Beyond economic implications, automation induces profound social changes, influencing everything from educational frameworks to leisure activities and family dynamics. As automation takes root, educational systems face pressure to adapt, prioritizing STEM subjects along with complementary skills to technology, such as critical thinking, creativity, and emotional intelligence. The demand for continuous learning and adaptability in the face of rapidly evolving job markets also becomes crucial, shaping a culture where lifelong learning is not just encouraged but necessary.

Moreover, as automation liberates individuals from routine tasks, it ostensibly offers more leisure time. However, the nature of this time and its impact on quality of life depend largely on social and economic contexts. For some, increased leisure could lead to greater engagement in community activities, hobbies, and personal development. For others, particularly those whose identities and social roles are tied closely to their professions, the transition may lead to a sense of loss and aimlessness, highlighting the need for social programs that address the psychological and social aspects of work displacement.

Policy Responses

Navigating the challenges presented by automation requires proactive policy responses that consider the multifaceted impacts on workers and society. One such policy is the implementation of a universal basic income (UBI), which proposes a periodic cash payment delivered to all citizens without means-testing or work requirements. UBI aims to provide a safety net for those displaced by automation, ensuring that everyone can afford basic necessities and helping to smooth the transition for workers as they adapt to the changing job landscape.

Retraining programs are another critical response aimed at equipping the workforce with new skills relevant to the evolving economic environment. These programs must be robust and accessible, offering training in high-demand areas such as digital literacy and technology management and sectors less likely to be affected by automation, such as healthcare and personal care.

Adjustments to labor laws are also necessary to protect workers in an automated economy. This might include redefining what constitutes work, ensuring fair wages for jobs augmented by technology, and regulating the gig economy to prevent exploitation.

Case Studies

Reflecting on real-world implementations offers valuable insights into the impact of automation. For instance, the automotive industry, one of the first adopters of automation technology, has seen significant transformations in manufacturing processes. Robotics and automated assembly lines have increased production rates and product consistency, reducing physical strain on workers. However, the reduction in demand for routine manual labor has shifted the skill set required, necessitating a workforce more adept in technology management and maintenance.

Another example can be found in the retail sector, where automation has revolutionized inventory management and customer service. Automated systems track product availability, optimize restocking processes, and even handle customer inquiries through chatbots. While these advancements have improved efficiency and customer experience, they have also led to job reductions for cashiers and salespeople, illustrating the need for retraining and transition programs for affected employees.

These case studies underline the dual narrative of automation: while it brings efficiency and growth, it also demands thoughtful consideration of the social and economic upheavals it may cause. The balance struck by policymakers, businesses, and society in responding to these changes will significantly shape the trajectory of our future economic and social structures.

6.3 Digital Nomadism: How Tech Enables Working from Anywhere

The concept of digital nomadism, where individuals use technology to work remotely and live an itinerant lifestyle, has seen a marked surge in both popularity and feasibility in recent years. At its core, this trend is underpinned by several key technologies that have made the digital nomad lifestyle accessible and sustainable. High-speed mobile internet access stands as the backbone of digital nomadism, providing the essential connectivity that enables remote work from almost anywhere on the globe. The advent of global 4G LTE and growing 5G networks has dramatically expanded the potential locales from which digital nomads can efficiently work, from bustling city cafés to tranquil beachfronts.

Moreover, the evolution of lightweight and powerful laptops has facilitated a mobile office setup that does not compromise on the capability or performance required for professional tasks. These devices are complemented by an array of global communication apps like Slack, Skype, and Zoom, which not only facilitate seamless collaboration with teams regardless of geographical boundaries but also maintain a sense of closeness and immediacy that is crucial for remote team dynamics. Additionally, cloud-based productivity tools such as Google Workspace and Microsoft 365 allow for real-time document collaboration and data synchronization across multiple devices, ensuring that digital nomads can work effectively from any location without the need for extensive hardware.

The lifestyle of digital nomads is characterized by a blend of work and travel, but achieving a balance between these aspects is not without its challenges. Managing work while exploring new cultures and environments requires a high degree of self-discipline and time management. Digital nomads often face the challenge of adapting to different time zones, which can disrupt work schedules and communication with clients or colleagues who are operating in a regular business-hours framework. Furthermore, finding reliable workspaces can be a significant hurdle, particularly in areas where infrastructure is less developed. Co-working spaces have emerged as a popular solution, offering not just a desk or office space but also an opportunity for networking and community engagement with other like-minded professionals.

The economic and social impacts of digital nomadism extend beyond the individuals themselves, influencing local communities and the broader global workforce. Economically, digital nomads can contribute to local economies by spending on accommodation, food, and entertainment. However, their presence can also lead to increased prices and living costs, potentially impacting local residents who might not share the same financial flexibility. Socially, the rise of digital nomadism challenges traditional notions of work and lifestyle, promoting a culture that values flexibility, autonomy, and the integration of work and life. This shift can inspire local populations to adopt new ways of working and living, although it also raises questions about long-term community cohesion and the integration of transient populations.

Looking forward, the future of digital nomadism is likely to be shaped by further technological advancements as well as evolving cultural and regulatory frameworks. Co-working spaces are anticipated to play an increasingly central role, not just as places to work but as hubs for innovation, collaboration, and social interaction. Governments are beginning to recognize the economic potential of attracting digital nomads, with countries like Estonia and Barbados introducing 'digital nomad visas' that allow foreigners to live and work remotely for extended periods. Such policies facilitate the nomadic lifestyle, help bridge cultural exchanges, and foster global connectivity.

As technology continues to advance, we can expect to see more sophisticated tools that make working remotely even more seamless. Innovations in virtual reality could transform remote collaboration, making interactions feel as natural and engaging as face-to-face meetings. AI-driven personal assistants could manage schedules and tasks more efficiently, allowing digital nomads to focus more on their work and less on the logistics of their lifestyle.

As digital nomadism continues to evolve, it stands as a testament to the transformative power of technology in reshaping not just how we work but also how we live and interact with the world. It offers a glimpse into a future where work is fully untethered from location, providing the freedom to design a lifestyle that aligns with individual preferences and aspirations. This shift is not merely about the technology that enables it but about the broader implications for society, culture, and the economy, challenging us to reimagine the possibilities of work and life in the digital age.

6.4 The Changing Landscape of Job Recruitment: AI in HR

The integration of Artificial Intelligence (AI) into human resources (HR) has marked a significant shift in how recruitment processes are conducted. Traditionally, the recruitment process was labor-intensive, involving manual screening of resumes, scheduling interviews, and following up on references. Today, AI technologies are reshaping this landscape, enhancing efficiency but also introducing new challenges and ethical concerns.

AI's role in recruitment primarily revolves around the automation of repetitive tasks. For example, AI-powered algorithms can quickly scan thousands of resumes to identify candidates whose skills and experiences match specific job descriptions. This capability accelerates the recruitment process and extends the reach of HR professionals by enabling them to evaluate a larger pool of applicants. Furthermore, AI-driven systems are employed to conduct initial interviews. Platforms equipped with natural language processing can interact with candidates via chatbots or virtual assistants, asking preliminary questions and gauging the responses. These systems analyze not just the content but also the sentiment and tone of the candidate's responses, providing insights that might go unnoticed in a traditional interview.

However, the use of AI in screening resumes and conducting interviews introduces potential biases that can perpetuate existing disparities in the hiring process. AI systems are only as unbiased as the data they are trained on. If the historical data used to train these algorithms contain biases, the AI will likely replicate them, possibly rejecting qualified candidates due to inherent prejudices in the training set. Recognizing these risks is crucial, and efforts are being made to develop AI tools that are transparent and fair. By incorporating diverse datasets and continuously monitoring outcomes for biases, organizations can mitigate some of the risks associated with AI in recruitment.

The evolution of AI in HR extends beyond operational efficiencies, fundamentally altering the role of human resources professionals. As routine tasks are automated, the focus of HR is shifting towards more strategic roles that require human judgment and expertise. This includes workforce planning, employee engagement, and talent retention strategies. However, this shift also necessitates the acquisition of new skills by HR professionals, including data literacy and an understanding of AI technologies. The ability to interpret data provided by AI tools and make informed decisions based on this analysis is becoming increasingly important. Moreover, as AI takes over more of the administrative duties, HR professionals are expected to take on roles that leverage their human skills, such as empathy and ethical judgment, which are crucial for addressing workforce concerns and maintaining an inclusive corporate culture.

Ethical considerations are paramount when integrating AI into recruitment. Privacy concerns arise as AI systems can access a vast amount of personal data about candidates. Ensuring that this data is handled securely and that candidates' privacy is respected is essential. As mentioned earlier, there is also the risk of discrimination, which can lead to legal and reputational risks. Organizations must ensure that their AI tools comply with relevant laws and ethical standards, which can involve regular audits and updates to AI systems to address any issues of fairness or bias.

Case Studies of AI Implementation

Several organizations have successfully integrated AI into their recruitment processes, illustrating both the potential benefits and challenges. One notable example is a multinational technology company that implemented an AI-driven recruitment system designed to streamline the hiring process. The system was programmed to scan resumes and identify top candidates based on criteria developed from successful employee profiles. Initially, the system delivered promising results, significantly reducing the time to hire and increasing the diversity of hires by expanding the recruitment funnel.

However, the company soon noticed that the AI system routinely overlooked certain qualified candidates. Further investigation revealed that the AI had inadvertently learned to replicate biases present in the historical data it was trained on. This led to a comprehensive review of the AI algorithms and training data, with a focus on eliminating biases. The company also instituted a hybrid model where AI recommendations were reviewed by human HR professionals to ensure fairness and accuracy in candidate selection.

Another example involves a healthcare provider that used AI to automate the scheduling of interviews and follow-up communications. This system not only improved the efficiency of the recruitment process but also enhanced the candidate experience by providing timely updates and feedback. The healthcare provider reported higher candidate satisfaction rates and was able to allocate more resources to strategic HR initiatives, such as employee development programs.

These case studies underscore AI's transformative impact on the recruitment process, highlighting the need for a balanced approach that leverages AI's efficiency while addressing the ethical and practical challenges it presents. As AI continues to evolve, its integration into HR practices will likely become more nuanced, reflecting a more profound understanding of its potential and limitations. This ongoing evolution will require continuous vigilance and adaptation by HR professionals, ensuring that recruitment practices meet the needs of the organization and uphold the principles of fairness and inclusivity.

6.5 Technology and the Evolution of Social Norms

The digital age has ushered in an era where the boundaries between the virtual and the real blur, reshaping our communication patterns in profound ways. The rise of digital communication platforms, from social media giants like Facebook and Twitter(X) to instant messaging apps such as WhatsApp and Telegram, has revolutionized how we interact with one another. These platforms enable instant connectivity with anyone across the globe, which, while opening up unprecedented avenues for networking and socialization, also shifts the dynamics of personal interactions. Previously, conversations were often confined to face-to-face interactions or voice calls, which inherently limited the scope and scale of communication. Now, digital communication facilitates a constant, pervasive flow of information and interaction that is accessible from anywhere at any time.

This shift has substantial implications for personal interactions. The convenience of digital communication comes at the cost of subtler nuances of human interaction that are often only conveyed through physical presence and vocal tones. Emojis and GIFs attempt to bridge this gap by adding layers of emotion and context, but they cannot fully replicate the depth of face-to-face interactions. Furthermore, the ease of communication that digital platforms provide can also lead to an overload of interactions, which can be both distracting and exhausting, a phenomenon often referred to as 'communication fatigue'. Despite these challenges, digital communication has become deeply integrated into our social fabric, influencing not just how we connect with others but also our expectations of accessibility and immediacy in communication.

The abundance of digital devices and platforms has also reshaped our privacy norms. In a world where sharing has become second nature, the lines between what is private and what is public have blurred. Social media platforms encourage users to share vast amounts of personal information online, from location data to intimate details of their personal lives. This shift has created a new social norm where the boundaries of privacy are continually negotiated and often pushed. The implications are double-edged; while some users feel empowered by the ability to share and connect, others are increasingly concerned about the erosion of personal privacy. Data breaches and scandals related to misuse of personal information have heightened these concerns, prompting calls for more stringent regulations on data privacy and a reevaluation of what we consider private in the digital age.

The impact of technology on social norms extends across generational divides, highlighting differences in technology adoption and usage that significantly influence societal structures and intergenerational relationships. Older generations often approach new technologies with caution and sometimes skepticism, preferring more traditional modes of communication and often valuing privacy more highly. In contrast, younger generations, particularly digital natives who have grown up with the internet and smartphones, are typically more adept at navigating digital platforms and more comfortable with the integration of technology into their daily lives. This divergence can lead to a 'digital divide' where different generations struggle to find common ground in their communication styles and perceptions of technology's role in society.

Looking forward, the trajectory of social norms is likely to continue evolving with the advancement of new technologies. Augmented reality (AR) and pervasive artificial intelligence (AI) are poised to further transform social interactions by integrating digital information with the physical world. AR, for example, could alter social interactions by overlaying digital data onto our real-world experiences, changing how we perceive and interact with our environment. Imagine walking through a city and seeing historical data or restaurant reviews overlaid on your field of vision, enhancing your interaction with your surroundings but also potentially distracting from the physical world.

Pervasive AI, as it becomes more integrated into our daily lives, could redefine norms around human-machine interactions. As AI agents become more sophisticated and capable of mimicking human behavior, the lines between human and machine interactions may become increasingly blurred. This integration raises profound questions about identity, privacy, and the nature of social relationships, challenging us to reconsider what it means to interact in a society where human and machine interactions are seamlessly intertwined.

As we navigate these changes, it is clear that technology is not merely a backdrop to societal evolution but a potent force actively shaping the fabric of our social norms. The challenge lies in balancing the benefits of these technological advancements with a mindful consideration of their broader implications for society.

6.6 Preparing Society for the Next Tech Wave

Educational Reforms

One of the most significant challenges in preparing society for the next wave of technological advancement lies in reforming educational systems to meet the demands of a future shaped by relentless innovation. The need for a robust educational framework that imparts knowledge and adapts to the dynamic tech landscape is crucial. Emphasizing STEM (science, technology, engineering, and mathematics) education is a foundational step, equipping students with the critical skills needed to navigate and innovate in a tech-driven world. However, the scope of educational reforms must extend beyond traditional STEM learning to include digital literacy—ensuring that all students, regardless of their future career paths, are proficient in understanding and leveraging digital tools.

The concept of lifelong learning is another pillar crucial to these reforms. In a world where technological advancements can render specific skills obsolete within a few years, the ability to continuously learn and adapt is invaluable. Educational institutions, therefore, must foster an environment that encourages continual learning beyond formal education. Initiatives might include offering modular courses, online learning platforms, and community workshops that allow individuals to acquire new skills as needed throughout their careers. By embedding these practices into the educational culture, society can cultivate a workforce that is resilient, adaptable, and prepared for the challenges of tomorrow.

Public Awareness and Engagement

As the pace of technological change accelerates, creating public awareness and engagement around these developments becomes imperative. This involves not only educating the public about the benefits and potentials of new technologies but also fostering a broad understanding of the implications these technologies may have on everyday life. Public seminars, tech fairs, and community programs can serve as platforms to demystify complex technologies like blockchain or AI, making them more accessible to the average person. Moreover, media outlets and educational platforms play a pivotal role in shaping public perception and knowledge, highlighting the need for responsible reporting and content creation that accurately reflects the opportunities and challenges posed by emerging technologies.

Engagement goes beyond awareness; it requires active participation from various segments of society in shaping the future of technology. This means providing avenues for public input on tech-related policies, encouraging community-led tech initiatives, and supporting grassroots innovations that address local needs. By involving diverse voices in the conversation, society can ensure that technological advancements are not only inclusive but also aligned with the broader public interest.

Collaboration Between Stakeholders

Navigating the future tech landscape necessitates unprecedented collaboration between various stakeholders, including governments, educational institutions, businesses, and civil society. This collaborative effort is essential to aligning the objectives and resources of these diverse groups towards a common goal: the sustainable and equitable integration of technology into society. Governments, for instance, can provide regulatory frameworks and incentives to support innovation while ensuring that tech developments benefit all citizens. Educational institutions, on their part, are crucial in researching and teaching the skills needed to thrive in a tech-driven future.

Businesses, particularly those at the forefront of technological innovation, can support educational initiatives through partnerships, funding, or collaborative research projects. Civil society organizations can act as bridges, connecting technology experts with the broader public to ensure that technological advancements are grounded in societal needs and ethical considerations. By working together, these stakeholders can create a synergistic ecosystem that supports sustainable technological advancement and prepares society for the changes it brings.

Scenario Planning

As a strategic tool, scenario planning can be invaluable in preparing for future technological impacts. This approach involves creating detailed, hypothetical scenarios based on possible future developments in technology. By exploring these scenarios, policymakers, business leaders, and other stakeholders can anticipate potential outcomes and challenges, allowing them to formulate strategies that are robust, flexible, and forward-thinking.

For instance, scenario planning can help a city prepare for the integration of autonomous vehicles, considering not only the technological and regulatory aspects but also the potential social and economic impacts.

Effective scenario planning requires a deep understanding of current trends, a creative outlook on future possibilities, and a commitment to revisiting and revising scenarios as new information becomes available. It encourages proactive rather than reactive strategies, enabling society to navigate the uncertainties of technological change with confidence and foresight.

As this chapter concludes, the themes of educational reform, public awareness, collaborative engagement, and strategic foresight merge to form a comprehensive approach to preparing society for the next tech wave. These elements underscore the multifaceted efforts required to not only harness technological advancements but also to ensure that these innovations contribute positively to societal progress. As we transition into the subsequent discussions, the focus shifts from preparation to action, exploring specific strategies and models that can facilitate the practical integration of these technologies into various sectors of society. The journey ahead, though fraught with challenges, offers unparalleled opportunities for innovation and growth, marking the next chapter in our continuous evolution alongside technology.

Chapter 7:
Forward-Thinking Insights

As we stand on the precipice of tomorrow, clutching the reins of today's technology, it's evident that the future is sculpted not just by the tools we have, but by the visions we dare to realize. The horizon of technological innovation is vibrant, pulsating with advancements that promise to redefine the boundaries of possibility. You, standing at this juncture, are not just a witness but a participant in this transformative era. This chapter delves into the technologies that are on the cusp of breaking through, their potential impacts across various sectors, and how you can strategically position yourself in this evolving landscape.

Emerging Technologies: Neuromorphic Computing and Advanced Materials for Energy Storage

The realm of emerging technologies is a fertile ground for innovation, where ideas that once flickered on the edges of imagination are nurtured into reality. Neuromorphic computing stands out as a revolutionary design that mimics the human brain's architecture, offering a new paradigm in processing efficiency and speed. This technology doesn't just process information; it learns and adapts, making it an ideal candidate for areas where cognitive flexibility and learning are crucial—such as autonomous vehicles and personalized medicine.

Simultaneously, the development of advanced materials for energy storage is breaking new ground. The quest for sustainable energy solutions has led to innovations like solid-state batteries, which promise higher energy density and safety compared to their lithium-ion counterparts. These advancements are crucial in a world inching towards renewable energy, as they offer the potential to store solar and wind energy more efficiently, thus solving one of the significant hurdles in the path of sustainable energy transition.

As of publication, the Chinese have managed to "grow" human brain cells from stem cells and integrate them onto a computer chip. More to come.

Impact Assessment: Healthcare, Energy, and Transportation

The ripple effects of neuromorphic computing and advanced energy storage materials are profound, particularly in sectors like healthcare, energy, and transportation. In healthcare, neuromorphic chips can power devices that adapt to various medical needs, learning from patient data to provide personalized diagnostics and treatments. Imagine a world where your medical devices adjust their functions to better suit your health conditions in real-time.

In the energy sector, advanced storage materials could lead to more robust and reliable grids capable of handling high loads from renewable sources without the risk of outages. This stability is paramount in ensuring that the transition to renewable energy is not just a temporary trend but a sustainable, long-term solution.

Both technologies could benefit the transportation sector immensely. Neuromorphic computing could enhance the decision-making capabilities of autonomous vehicles, making them safer and more efficient. Meanwhile, advanced energy storage solutions could extend the range of electric vehicles, accelerating their adoption and consequently reducing their carbon footprints.

Investment Opportunities: Identifying and Evaluating

As these technologies advance, they open a panorama of investment opportunities. For you, the savvy investor or the curious entrepreneur, understanding where to place your resources requires a keen eye for potential and an in-depth understanding of technological trajectories. Investing in companies that produce neuromorphic chips or develop advanced materials for energy storage can be lucrative. However, it demands due diligence and a strategic approach to risk assessment. Evaluate the market readiness of these technologies, the regulatory landscape, and the competitive environment to make informed investment decisions.

Preparation Strategies: Integration in Business Operations

For businesses and professionals, preparing for the integration of breakthrough technologies involves strategic foresight and adaptability. Companies should consider establishing innovation hubs or partnerships with tech startups to stay ahead of the curve. Training programs that upskill employees to work with new technologies like neuromorphic computing can be a game-changer, ensuring that your workforce is not rendered obsolete but is empowered to ride the wave of innovation.

Moreover, businesses should engage in scenario planning to anticipate how these technologies might disrupt their industries. By understanding potential outcomes, you can develop flexible business models that adapt to rapid technological changes, securing a competitive advantage in a future where change is the only constant.

Navigating this complex yet exhilarating landscape of emerging technologies requires your role to extend beyond passive observation to active participation. Whether you are an investor, a business leader, or a technology enthusiast, your actions and decisions will contribute to shaping the future. As these technologies evolve, they offer not just challenges but also opportunities to redefine industries, enhance human capabilities, and pave the way for a future that resonates with the promise of innovation and the potential for extraordinary achievements.

Ethical AI Development: Guidelines and Best Practices

In the labyrinth of technological evolution, artificial intelligence (AI) emerges as a beacon of potential and a source of ethical conundrum.

As you navigate this domain, understanding and implementing ethical frameworks is not merely an academic exercise but a crucial practice to ensure the responsible development of AI technologies. Ethical AI isn't just about preventing harm; it's about fostering trust and advancing technology in ways that benefit all of society.

Developing Ethical Frameworks

The cornerstone of ethical AI involves the establishment of frameworks that encompass fairness, transparency, and accountability. Fairness ensures that AI systems do not perpetuate biases or discriminate, which requires a meticulous design process that actively identifies and mitigates potential biases in training data and algorithms. Transparency in AI conveys how and why decisions are made by an AI system, necessitating clear documentation and communication of AI processes and functionalities. This is critical not only for user trust but also for regulatory compliance. Accountability in AI assigns responsibility for the outcomes of AI behavior, ensuring that there are mechanisms in place to audit and modify AI systems when they fail or produce unintended consequences.

For you, engaging with these frameworks means advocating for and adopting practices that adhere to legal standards and exceed them, championing ethical considerations as foundational to your operational ethos. It involves regular ethical audits and the willingness to recalibrate strategies in response to emerging ethical insights.

Best Practices in Implementation

Implementing ethical AI effectively requires a commitment to best practices that extend throughout the lifecycle of AI systems. One fundamental practice is the composition of diverse teams. Diversity in AI development teams is not just a token of inclusivity but a critical factor in broadening perspectives and reducing unconscious biases that might manifest in AI systems. Such teams bring varied experiences and viewpoints that are invaluable in identifying potential ethical pitfalls and innovating more equitable AI solutions.

Continuous monitoring of AI systems is another best practice that cannot be overstated. AI systems, by design, learn and evolve based on new data. Continuous monitoring ensures that changes in AI behavior remain aligned with ethical standards and that any deviations are addressed promptly. This includes implementing robust mechanisms for feedback and redress, allowing users to report concerns, and ensuring these concerns are used to improve AI systems.

Global Standards and Regulations

The call for global standards and regulations in AI ethics underscores the need for a cohesive and unified approach to managing AI's global impact. Just as cyber threats know no borders, AI's implications are boundless. Global standards ensure that AI systems can operate across national boundaries without ethical discrepancies, providing a consistent framework that protects users and informs developers.

Engaging with international bodies to shape these standards is crucial. It involves active participation in global forums and regulatory discussions to advocate for ethical guidelines that are both rigorous and adaptable. These standards should reflect a consensus among diverse stakeholders, including technologists, ethicists, policymakers, and the public, ensuring that they are comprehensive and practicable.

Case Studies

Real-world applications of ethical AI guidelines offer tangible insights into their efficacy. For instance, a European tech company implemented an AI system for credit scoring. By adhering to ethical guidelines, they ensured the system provided explanations for credit denials, allowing individuals to understand and contest decisions. This transparency enhanced customer trust and ensured compliance with the EU's General Data Protection Regulation (GDPR).

Another case involves a U.S.-based healthcare provider that used AI to optimize patient treatment plans. By assembling a diverse team, including medical professionals, ethicists, and patients, the company developed an AI system that accounted for a wide range of health determinants while ensuring the protection of sensitive patient data. Continuous monitoring allowed the system to adapt to new health data, improving accuracy and efficacy in patient care without compromising ethical standards.

These cases exemplify how ethical AI development is not just about preventing negative outcomes but also about enhancing AI's positive impacts on society. By adhering to established ethical frameworks, implementing best practices, and engaging in the creation of global standards, you ensure that AI serves as a tool for societal benefit, framed by a commitment to ethical integrity and human-centric values.

Protecting Against the Next Generation of Cyber Threats

In the digital microcosm where advancements unfold at an accelerating pace, the shadows loom equally large, with cyber threats morphing with each technological leap. As you stand vigilant in this ever-evolving landscape, understanding and deploying advanced cybersecurity technologies becomes crucial. Quantum encryption and AI-driven threat detection systems represent the frontier of cybersecurity, offering robust defenses against increasingly sophisticated cyberattacks. Quantum encryption, for instance, leverages the principles of quantum mechanics to create secure communications that are theoretically impenetrable by any conventional hacking methods. This technology uses the quantum properties of particles to create cryptographic keys shared between senders and receivers, making the encrypted message impossible to intercept without detection.

Simultaneously, AI-driven threat detection systems use machine learning algorithms to analyze patterns and predict potential threats with speed and accuracy far beyond human capabilities. These systems continuously learn from new data, adapting to new threats in real-time and providing a dynamic defense mechanism that evolves with the threat landscape itself. For instance, these AI systems can detect anomalies in network traffic that might indicate a breach or identify phishing attempts that could elude traditional detection methods. The integration of AI in cybersecurity not only enhances the ability to respond to threats but also anticipates them, shifting the paradigm from reactive to proactive security measures.

As the cyber threat landscape evolves, so do the nature and complexity of the threats. Cybercriminals now utilize AI and machine learning to develop more sophisticated hacking techniques, such as polymorphic malware that can change its code to avoid detection or deepfake technology used to create realistic audio and video hoaxes. The proliferation of IoT devices further expands the attack surface, providing new vectors for cyberattacks. These devices, often lacking robust security features, can serve as entry points to wider network infrastructures, making entire systems vulnerable to exploitation.

To combat these emerging threats, both individuals and organizations must adopt a comprehensive suite of preventative measures and strategies. For individuals, this involves basic cyber hygiene practices such as using strong, unique passwords for different accounts, enabling two-factor authentication, and regularly updating software to patch security vulnerabilities. Organizations, on the other hand, need to implement more sophisticated measures, such as conducting regular security audits, employing endpoint detection and response (EDR) systems, and training employees in cybersecurity awareness. These practices help in identifying vulnerabilities, monitoring for threats, and educating users on the importance of security, forming the first line of defense against cyberattacks.

Building cyber resilience extends beyond technological solutions to encompass a broader strategy that includes education, policy, and community engagement. Cyber resilience is about creating systems that are not only protected against attacks but are also prepared to respond and recover if compromised. This involves developing a cyber-resilient culture where cybersecurity is integrated into the fabric of organizational operations and decision-making processes. Policies that promote data protection, incident response plans, and recovery strategies are essential components of a resilient framework. Moreover, collaboration between industry, academia, and government can foster innovation in cybersecurity solutions and policies, ensuring a unified response to cyber threats.

Educational initiatives play a pivotal role in building cyber resilience. By incorporating cybersecurity education at all levels—from schools to corporate training programs—individuals become equipped with the knowledge and skills necessary to navigate the cyber landscape safely. Public awareness campaigns can also play a significant role in informing the wider community about the risks and precautions associated with digital activities. These educational efforts should aim to demystify cybersecurity, making it accessible and understandable to everyone, thereby empowering individuals and organizations to take proactive steps in protecting their digital environments.

As you navigate this complex domain, remember that the goal is not just to defend against known threats but to anticipate and prepare for future challenges. In a world where technology connects and permeates every aspect of our lives, creating robust cyber defenses is not a luxury but a necessity, ensuring that our digital journeys continue unimpeded by the shadows that lurk in the background.

The Role of AI in Future Global Diplomacy

In the intricate dance of international relations, where every word and gesture carries weight, artificial intelligence (AI) is poised to revolutionize the way nations interact and negotiate. AI's potential as a diplomatic tool extends beyond mere computational efficiency; it offers a transformative approach to understanding and managing the complex dynamics of global diplomacy. As you explore this evolving landscape, consider how AI could enhance strategic decision-making and foster international cooperation in ways previously unimaginable.

AI's capability to simulate and predict outcomes of international negotiations could provide diplomats with unprecedented strategic advantages. By processing vast amounts of data, including historical treaties, economic reports, and real-time communications, AI models can identify patterns and predict negotiation outcomes with high accuracy. This predictive power enables diplomats to enter negotiations with a clear understanding of potential responses and the likely impact of their proposals. For instance, AI could simulate a range of scenarios based on different negotiation strategies, helping diplomats choose the approach that maximizes national interests while maintaining international harmony.

The ethical considerations of employing AI in such a sensitive and impactful context are, however, profound. Transparency in how AI models are used in diplomatic contexts is crucial to maintaining trust among nations. There is a fine line between leveraging AI for strategic advantage and manipulating negotiations in a way that could lead to accusations of unfairness or covert influence. Ensuring that AI systems are designed and operated transparently is essential to prevent their misuse and to foster an environment of mutual trust and respect among international partners. Ethical guidelines and oversight mechanisms must be established to govern the use of AI in diplomacy, ensuring that all actions are in line with international laws and norms.

Moreover, AI holds the potential to significantly enhance communication between nations by overcoming language barriers and cultural differences. Advanced natural language processing (NLP) systems and real-time translation services powered by AI can remove linguistic obstacles that have traditionally impeded diplomatic interactions. These technologies allow for smoother, clearer communication, ensuring that nuances and subtleties are not lost in translation. Furthermore, AI-driven analysis of cultural nuances can help diplomats understand and respect international partners' cultural contexts, which is often critical in building and maintaining diplomatic relationships.

Looking to the future, AI is likely to become a central element in global diplomacy and international relations. We can envision scenarios where AI systems facilitate negotiations and help manage complex international crises by providing real-time data and analysis, enabling quicker and more informed decision-making. In peacekeeping missions, AI could be used to monitor developments on the ground, analyze risks, and provide recommendations for intervention strategies that minimize conflict and promote stability. As nations navigate the challenges of global governance, AI could become an indispensable ally in promoting peace, justice, and international cooperation.

As you integrate AI into the realm of international diplomacy, it is imperative to proceed with both ambition and caution. The fusion of technology and diplomatic strategy opens new avenues for advancing global dialogues and understanding, paving the way for a more interconnected and harmonious world. However, this new frontier also calls for a renewed commitment to ethical standards and international collaboration to ensure that AI serves as a force for good, enhancing diplomatic efforts without compromising the values of equity and mutual respect that are the foundation of international relations.

7.5 Future Technologies in Education: What Comes Next?

The landscape of education is undergoing a metamorphosis, driven by technological innovations that tailor learning experiences to the individual needs of students and transcend traditional classroom boundaries. At the forefront are AI-driven personalized learning platforms, which have begun to redefine educational paradigms by offering customized learning experiences that adapt to the pace and style of each student. These platforms utilize sophisticated algorithms to analyze students' learning patterns, preferences, and performance, enabling them to present educational content in ways that maximize understanding and retention. For instance, an AI system might detect a student's difficulty in grasping a particular concept and subsequently alter the teaching approach, perhaps by introducing interactive elements or providing additional resources tailored to the student's learning style. This level of personalization enhances academic performance and fosters a deeper engagement with the learning material, potentially igniting lifelong passions for specific subjects.

The integration of augmented reality (AR) into educational settings further exemplifies how technology is transforming the learning environment. AR has the potential to provide immersive experiences that make abstract or complex subjects more tangible and engaging. Imagine a biology class where students can visualize cellular processes in 3D right on their desks, or a history lesson where they can witness historical events unfold in real-time in the middle of the classroom. These experiences, powered by AR, enhance understanding and increase student engagement by making learning an interactive and enjoyable activity. The potential for AR in education extends beyond just visual aids; it offers new ways to interact with knowledge, transforming passive learning into an active exploration that captivates students' imaginations and curiosity.

Blockchain technology also presents a significant opportunity in the realm of education, particularly in the verification and storage of educational credentials. With blockchain, academic records and credentials can be stored in a secure, immutable ledger accessible by educational institutions and employers globally without the risk of tampering or fraud. This system simplifies the process of qualification recognition, making it easier for students to pursue opportunities across borders and for employers to verify the qualifications of potential hires confidently. The transparency and security offered by blockchain streamline administrative processes and enhance trust in the credentials issued by educational institutions, potentially transforming global education and employment landscapes.

The role of big data in education cannot be overstressed. Through the analysis of large datasets encompassing student behaviors, learning outcomes, and even social interactions, educators and administrators can gain valuable insights into the effectiveness of teaching methods and curricular designs. Big data enables a level of analysis that is both broad and deep, offering previously unattainable perspectives. By understanding patterns in student performance across different demographics and learning environments, educational institutions can implement targeted improvements and innovations that address specific needs, thereby elevating the overall quality of education. Moreover, the predictive power of big data analytics could lead to the proactive identification of at-risk students, allowing for timely interventions that could dramatically alter educational outcomes and reduce dropout rates.

As you navigate this evolving educational landscape, the convergence of these technologies offers a glimpse into a future where learning is deeply personalized, highly interactive, and securely managed. The traditional boundaries of classrooms are expanding, ushered forward by innovations that not only transform how knowledge is delivered and experienced but also how it is validated and utilized across global platforms. The integration of AI, AR, blockchain, and big data in education is not merely a trend but a profound shift towards a more inclusive, engaging, and accountable educational system that is equipped to meet the challenges and opportunities of the 21st century. As these technologies continue to develop and intersect, they promise to further revolutionize the educational experience, making learning a more personalized, immersive, and universally accessible journey for students around the world.

7.6 The Intersection of Tech and Leisure: Future Trends in Travel

As we contemplate the future of travel, technology emerges as a transformative force, reshaping the landscape of tourism with innovations that promise not only enhanced experiences but also greater sustainability and security. The convergence of virtual reality (VR), artificial intelligence (AI), and other technological advancements is not merely altering how we travel but also redefining the possibilities of exploring the world. This evolution in travel tech offers you, the modern traveler, an unprecedented ability to experience the world in ways that are both deeply personal and expansively global.

Technology-enhanced tourism now allows you to immerse yourself in VR travel experiences that transcend physical boundaries. Imagine donning a VR headset and walking through the bustling markets of Marrakech or the serene landscapes of Iceland, all from the comfort of your home. These VR experiences are meticulously crafted using real-world data and high-resolution imaging, providing a sensory-rich exploration that rivals physical travel.

Beyond leisure, these technologies serve educational purposes, allowing students and curious minds to explore historical sites and natural wonders without geographical constraints. AI further personalizes this experience by curating itineraries based on your preferences and past travel behaviors, suggesting destinations and experiences most likely to captivate your interest.

In the realm of sustainable travel technologies, the industry is witnessing significant advancements that align with global sustainability goals. Electric aircraft, for instance, are on the horizon, promising to reduce the carbon footprint of air travel by utilizing electric motors instead of fossil fuels. Although currently in the developmental phase, these aircraft could revolutionize air travel by making it cleaner and more energy-efficient. Similarly, smart, energy-efficient accommodations are becoming increasingly popular, leveraging IoT technology to minimize energy use and reduce waste. Hotels equipped with smart thermostats, automated lighting systems, and water-saving technologies offer enhanced comfort and convenience and ensure that your travel has a minimal environmental impact.

Security and convenience are paramount in today's travel industry, with technologies like biometric verification and real-time luggage tracking enhancing both aspects. Biometric systems use unique identifiers such as fingerprints, facial recognition, or retinal scans to streamline security processes at airports, reducing wait times and enhancing passenger throughput without compromising security. Real-time luggage tracking, enabled by IoT devices, allows you to monitor the status and location of your luggage through a smartphone app, providing peace of mind and significantly reducing the incidence of lost luggage. These technologies, by simplifying and securing travel logistics, allow you to navigate through airports and transit systems with ease and confidence.

The COVID-19 pandemic has indelibly marked the travel industry, accelerating the adoption of health monitoring and contactless services. Health monitoring devices, integrated with AI systems, can now predict potential health risks by analyzing data from a range of sources, including wearable health monitors and global health databases. This capability could allow for real-time health advisories and personalized travel recommendations based on current health conditions and outbreaks. Contactless services, from automated check-ins at airports to touchless payments in hotels and restaurants, have become the norm. These services reduce physical contact and streamline operations, making travel smoother and safer.

As technology advances, the intersection of tech and leisure will likely continue to evolve, offering new ways to enhance, secure, and personalize travel experiences. The future of travel looks promising, with technological innovations making it more immersive, sustainable, and convenient. As a traveler in this evolving landscape, you stand to benefit from an array of technologies that transform how you experience the world and ensure that your adventures are as responsible as they are memorable.

7.7 Blockchain and Its Future Applications in Society

In the ever-expanding universe of digital innovation, blockchain technology emerges not merely as a foundation for cryptocurrencies but as a transformative architecture with the potential to redefine transparency and efficiency in numerous non-financial sectors. As you explore the broader applications of blockchain, consider its implications in areas like supply chain management, voting systems, and real estate transactions. These sectors stand to benefit immensely from the decentralized, immutable, and transparent nature of blockchain technology, which ensures that every transaction or exchange is recorded securely and indelibly.

Blockchain's application in supply chain management revolutionizes how goods are tracked from production to delivery.

Traditional supply chains often suffer from opacity that can lead to inefficiencies, fraud, and counterfeiting. Blockchain introduces a level of transparency that allows every participant in the supply chain to view the history and status of a product, from raw materials to final delivery, in real-time. This not only enhances trust among stakeholders but also enables the precise pinpointing of inefficiencies and fraud. For instance, consider a scenario where a blockchain system tracks the journey of pharmaceuticals; stakeholders can verify the authenticity of drugs at every stage, significantly reducing the risk of counterfeit medications entering the supply chain, thus safeguarding consumer health and corporate integrity.

Moreover, the realm of democratic processes and voting systems can be profoundly optimized by blockchain technology. Traditional voting systems, fraught with challenges related to security, voter privacy, and integrity, can be revolutionized through blockchain's capacity to create a secure and transparent digital ledger of votes. By ensuring that each vote is anonymously but immutably recorded, blockchain can eliminate common issues such as double voting or vote tampering. Imagine a future where election results are instantly verifiable and universally trusted without the need for recounts or fears of manipulation. This application streamlines the voting process and enhances democratic participation by bolstering voter confidence in the electoral system.

In the real estate sector, blockchain can simplify transactions by reducing the layers of bureaucracy and the risk of fraud associated with property transactions. Each property's history, including past transactions, liens, and ownership, can be securely recorded on a blockchain, providing potential buyers with accessible and tamper-proof property records. This transparency significantly speeds up the buying process, reduces the costs associated with title searches and insurance, and increases trust in property transactions. Furthermore, blockchain enables the tokenization of real estate assets, allowing them to be traded similarly to stocks on an exchange, thereby increasing liquidity and opening up investment opportunities to a broader range of investors.

While blockchain's benefits are compelling, several challenges and limitations must be addressed to realize its full potential across these sectors. Technologically, scalability remains a significant challenge; the current capacity of blockchain systems to handle large-scale transactions efficiently is still under development. Additionally, the energy consumption associated with blockchain, particularly systems that use proof-of-work consensus mechanisms, poses environmental concerns that need to be mitigated to ensure the sustainable growth of blockchain technologies.

From a regulatory perspective, the decentralized nature of blockchain poses a unique challenge. Regulatory frameworks that govern traditional transactions and industries may not be directly applicable to decentralized systems, necessitating the development of new regulations that understand and accommodate the nuances of blockchain. Moreover, the global nature of blockchain requires international cooperation to establish cross-border regulatory standards and prevent issues such as tax evasion and money laundering.

Looking ahead, predictive scenarios for blockchain technology paint a transformative landscape for various aspects of society. In the next few decades, we might see blockchain being used to create a global digital identity for individuals, which could be used to secure and streamline processes ranging from healthcare access and banking to cross-border travel and voting, fundamentally altering how personal identity is managed and utilized in a digital world. In healthcare, blockchain could enable the creation of universal health records that are secure, easily accessible by authorized personnel regardless of geographical location, and updated in real-time, greatly enhancing the efficiency and quality of healthcare delivery.

As blockchain continues to evolve, its potential to reshape various facets of society becomes increasingly evident. This technology holds the promise not only of enhanced efficiency and security but also of fostering a more equitable and transparent global society. As you engage with blockchain, whether as a developer, investor, or consumer, you are participating in the unfolding of a technological revolution that could redefine the foundational structures of our digital age, paving the way for innovations that integrate security, transparency, and efficiency at their core.

7.8 The Future of Digital Identity Verification

The digital age necessitates a paradigm shift in how we conceive and verify identity, ushering in sophisticated technologies that redefine security, efficiency, and access. Advancements in digital identity technologies, particularly biometric authentication and blockchain-based identity systems, are at the forefront of this transformation. Biometric authentication uses unique physical characteristics, such as fingerprints, facial recognition, and iris scans, to verify individuals' identities with a high degree of accuracy and minimal intrusion. This technology has been integrated widely, from unlocking smartphones to securing access to high-security facilities, reflecting its reliability and user-friendly nature. On the other hand, blockchain-based identity systems offer a decentralized approach to identity verification, storing personal data across a network of computers that makes it nearly impervious to fraud and theft. These systems provide users with control over their digital identities, allowing them to share information selectively and securely, free from the oversight of a central authority.

However, the integration of these advanced technologies into everyday life raises significant privacy and security concerns. The balance between convenience and privacy is a delicate one; biometric data, if compromised, can be particularly damaging because, unlike passwords, biometric traits are permanently linked to users and cannot be changed. The potential for misuse of this data by corporations or governments could lead to unprecedented levels of surveillance and control over individuals. Blockchain technology, while enhancing security by decentralizing data storage, also poses risks if not implemented with strong encryption and privacy safeguards. Moreover, the permanence of blockchain records means that once personal information is logged, it is challenging to alter or delete, which could conflict with privacy rights, such as the right to be forgotten.

Regulatory perspectives on digital identity verification are evolving as governments attempt to keep pace with technological advancements. The widespread adoption of digital identity systems raises complex regulatory issues that span privacy, data protection, and cross-border identity recognition. Regulations such as the General Data Protection Regulation (GDPR) in the European Union provide a framework for protecting personal data within digital identity systems, mandating strict guidelines on data consent and user control. However, global consensus on digital identity standards is lacking, leading to a fragmented regulatory landscape that can hinder the international interoperability of identity verification systems. This lack of uniformity can be particularly challenging for multinational corporations and global initiatives that depend on consistent identity verification methods across borders.

The global impact of universally accepted digital identity systems could be transformative, particularly for underserved populations. In regions where proof of identity is a barrier to accessing essential services, such as banking, healthcare, and voting, digital identity systems can unlock opportunities and foster greater inclusion. For instance, in remote or impoverished areas where traditional forms of ID may be difficult to obtain or prove, a mobile-based digital ID can provide individuals with the means to establish their identity reliably and access services that are crucial for economic and social development. Furthermore, digital identities can facilitate the seamless movement of people across borders, enhancing global mobility and connectivity in an increasingly interconnected world.

As we advance further into the digital frontier, the role of technology in shaping our identity and interactions continues to grow. The development and deployment of digital identity verification technologies must be guided by a commitment to security, privacy, and inclusiveness, ensuring that these innovations empower rather than undermine the individuals they are designed to protect. As you navigate this evolving landscape, staying informed and engaged with the ongoing discourse on digital identity is crucial for harnessing its benefits while safeguarding against its risks, thereby contributing to a future where technology and identity intersect in ways that enhance, rather than compromise, our human experience.

7.9 Innovations in 3D Printing: Industrial and Personal Use

The evolution of 3D printing technology has ushered in a new era of manufacturing, characterized by its ability to streamline production processes and catalyze innovation across various industries. At the forefront of this revolution are groundbreaking developments in 3D printing materials and methods, such as metal printing and bioprinting, which expand the utility and applicability of this technology far beyond its initial scope. Metal printing, for instance, has transformed from a prototyping tool to a full-fledged production technique that can produce complex, high-strength metal parts with precision. This method is increasingly employed in sectors that demand high performance and customization, such as aerospace and automotive manufacturing, where components often require intricate designs and superior mechanical properties.

Bioprinting represents another significant advancement, utilizing a similar layer-by-layer approach to create tissue-like structures that mimic natural biological systems. This technique holds immense potential in the medical field, offering prospects for creating personalized organs or tissue models for pharmaceutical testing. The ability to print biological materials is not just a technological triumph but a beacon of hope for millions who await organ transplants or suffer from diseases that could benefit from personalized therapeutic treatments. As you delve deeper into the capabilities of 3D printing, it becomes evident that this technology is not merely about shaping plastic and metal but about forging new pathways in human health and recovery.

The impact of 3D printing on customization and production is profound and widespread, touching industries ranging from healthcare to automotive and even reaching into personal-use markets. The allure of 3D printing lies in its capacity to tailor products to individual specifications without the need for expensive molds or tooling. This capability not only democratizes manufacturing, allowing small businesses and even individuals to bring unique products to market at a fraction of traditional costs but also significantly reduces the time from design to production. For example, automotive companies utilize 3D printing to create custom parts for limited edition vehicles, while medical professionals use it to produce bespoke prosthetics tailored to the specific anatomical measurements of their patients. This level of customization is transforming traditional production paradigms, shifting the focus from mass production to mass customization, where the needs and preferences of the individual take center stage.

However, the environmental impact of 3D printing is a topic of intense scrutiny and debate. On one hand, 3D printing can reduce waste by using only the amount of material necessary to build a part, unlike subtractive manufacturing processes that cut away significant portions of materials. Additionally, the ability to produce parts on-demand can decrease the need for transporting goods over long distances, thus reducing the carbon footprint associated with logistics. On the other hand, concerns about the energy consumption of 3D printers and the recyclability of printing materials pose challenges to the sustainability of this technology. Addressing these environmental impacts requires ongoing research into more sustainable materials and more energy-efficient printing processes, ensuring that 3D printing can grow without exacerbating the planet's ecological crises.

Looking to the future, the applications of 3D printing technology appear almost limitless. In space exploration, for instance, NASA is already experimenting with 3D printers that can produce spare parts on demand for spacecraft, reducing the need for carrying large numbers of spare parts on missions, which can be costly and space-consuming. The potential for building habitats on other planets using materials found on-site, a process known as in-situ resource utilization, could dramatically change the economics of space colonization. Closer to home, the burgeoning field of human augmentation explores the use of 3D printing to enhance human capabilities beyond their natural physiological limits. From exoskeletons designed to boost strength and endurance to implants that enhance sensory perceptions, 3D printing stands at the confluence of human aspiration and technological innovation.

As you engage with the world of 3D printing, it becomes clear that this technology is not just a tool for creating objects but a driving force capable of redefining the boundaries of what is possible in manufacturing, medicine, and beyond. The journey from the macro to the micro, from large-scale industrial uses to personalized applications, reveals a technology that is versatile, dynamic, and poised to play a critical role in shaping the future of human-technology interaction. Whether in the creation of a satellite part that can withstand the harsh conditions of space or a medical implant tailored to the physiological needs of a patient, 3D printing stands ready to meet the challenges of the modern world with innovation and adaptability at its core.

7.10 Virtual Reality Therapy: The Future of Mental Health Treatment

The therapeutic realm is witnessing a profound transformation with the integration of virtual reality (VR) technology, particularly in the treatment of conditions such as post-traumatic stress disorder (PTSD), anxiety, and various phobias. This innovative approach leverages the immersive power of VR to create controlled environments where patients can confront and work through their fears in a safe and controlled setting. Unlike traditional therapy methods, which often rely on patients' ability to use their imagination to revisit distressing experiences, VR therapy places individuals directly into a virtual environment that can be closely monitored and adjusted by therapists.

For patients dealing with PTSD, VR allows for careful and measured re-exposure to trauma-related cues, enabling them to process and manage their reactions in a supportive environment. Therapists can tailor the virtual scenarios to each individual's experiences, gradually increasing the intensity of the exposure as the patient becomes better able to cope with their trauma. This method is grounded in established therapeutic principles such as cognitive-behavioral therapy (CBT), providing a new tool that enhances traditional techniques with the precision and engagement of immersive technology. Similarly, individuals suffering from phobias such as fear of flying or heights can benefit from gradual exposure in a virtual environment, which can help to dismantle the fear response in a way that feels real yet remains entirely controlled and reversible.

The benefits of VR therapy extend beyond its efficacy in exposure treatments. This form of therapy can generate a sense of presence that is often more challenging to achieve through traditional therapeutic methods. The immersive nature of VR provides a compelling and engaging environment for patients, which can be particularly useful in treating younger populations or those who might find traditional therapy settings intimidating or abstract. Moreover, VR allows for sessions to be replicated exactly, ensuring consistency in therapeutic settings, which is crucial for research and treatment standardization.

Despite the promising advantages, the adoption of VR therapy faces significant challenges related to cost, accessibility, and standardization. The high cost of VR equipment and the need for specialized software and trained personnel can limit the availability of VR therapy primarily to well-funded clinics or research institutions. This poses a significant barrier to widespread adoption, as individuals who could benefit from such treatments might not have access due to geographic or economic constraints. Additionally, the therapeutic community has yet to establish standardized protocols for the use of VR in clinical settings, which is necessary to ensure that treatments are delivered safely and effectively across different practitioners and patients.

Future Developments in VR Therapy

Looking ahead, the future of VR therapy is poised for significant advancements as the technology becomes more integrated with artificial intelligence (AI) and biofeedback systems. The integration of AI can lead to personalized treatment plans that adapt in real-time to a patient's responses within the virtual environment. For instance, AI algorithms can analyze data from a patient's performance during therapy sessions to optimize and individualize their treatment plan, enhancing the efficacy of the therapy. Real-time biofeedback, which monitors physiological responses such as heart rate and skin conductance, can provide immediate metrics on a patient's reaction to therapy, allowing therapists to fine-tune the virtual environment and therapeutic approach dynamically.

The potential of VR to revolutionize mental health treatment is immense, offering tools that blend the best of technology and psychology. As research continues to unfold, it is anticipated that VR will become an increasingly common and effective tool in psychological treatments, making therapy more accessible, engaging, and precise. As this technology develops, it will be crucial for ongoing collaboration between technologists, therapists, and regulatory bodies to address the challenges of cost, accessibility, and protocol standardization, ensuring that VR therapy can reach its full potential in clinical practice.

This exploration of VR therapy not only highlights its current applications and benefits but also sets the stage for future innovations that could further revolutionize the field of mental health treatment. As we continue to navigate the complexities of psychological disorders, the integration of advanced technologies such as VR offers new hope and possibilities for patient care, opening doors to treatments that are as compassionate as they are cutting-edge.

Conclusion

As we draw the curtains on this exploration of technology and future trends, it is essential to revisit the journey we have embarked upon together. From the evolution of artificial intelligence to the transformative potential of blockchain and quantum computing, we have traversed the complex landscape of rapidly advancing technologies. These developments, as highlighted throughout this book, are not merely shaping our tools but are fundamentally reshaping our societal structures, our economies, and our personal lives.

The importance of ethical considerations in technology cannot be overstated. As we have discussed, every innovation carries with it questions of privacy, security, and the broader impacts on society. It is imperative that, as creators, users, and regulators, we ensure that technology is developed and implemented responsibly. Our commitment must be to foster innovations that prioritize human welfare and lead to a fair and equitable society.

Throughout this book, we have seen how technology holds the keys to addressing some of the most pressing global challenges. From combating climate change through advanced climate modeling and sustainable tech innovations to revolutionizing healthcare with telemedicine and AI-driven diagnostics, technology offers us tools of unprecedented power. These examples serve not only as a testament to human ingenuity but also as a call to action to harness these advancements for the greater good.

The landscape of technology is ever-changing, and keeping pace requires an ongoing commitment to learning and adaptation. I urge you, the reader, to remain curious and proactive, embracing a lifelong journey of education and discovery. The future will be shaped by those who are prepared to navigate its complexities and seize its opportunities.

I call upon you to engage proactively with the technology around you. Participate in discussions, contribute to ethical tech initiatives, or pursue a career that advances responsible technology. Your actions can influence how technology is shaped and implemented in our societies.

Looking ahead, I am hopeful about the future we can create—a future where technology and humanity converge in harmony, leading to sustainable, equitable, and innovative global communities. I encourage you to view yourself as an integral part of this exciting trajectory. Reflect on your relationship with technology—how you use it, how you are affected by it, and how you can influence its development.

Finally, I invite you to join the broader conversation about technology's role in our future. Engage with online communities, attend tech talks, or participate in forums where ideas and innovations are shared and debated. Your voice is crucial in the collective endeavor to ensure that technology serves as a force for good.

Together, let us step forward into a future where technology promises greater capabilities and upholds our shared values and aspirations. Thank you for joining me on this journey, and may you continue to explore, learn, and influence the world around you with the thoughtful application of technology.

References

- *Ethical concerns mount as AI takes bigger decision-making* ...
  https://news.harvard.edu/gazette/story/2020/10/ethical-concerns-mount-as-ai-takes-bigger-decision-making-role/

- *35 Amazing Real World Examples Of How Blockchain Is* ...
  https://bernardmarr.com/35-amazing-real-world-examples-of-how-blockchain-is-changing-our-world/

- *Recent advances in CRISPR-based functional genomics* ...
  https://www.nature.com/articles/s12276-024-01212-3

- *Quantum science and technology: highlights of 2023*
  https://physicsworld.com/a/quantum-science-and-technology-highlights-of-2023/

- *The Evolution of Smart Home Technology*
  https://blog.bccresearch.com/the-evolution-of-smart-home-technology

- *The Impact of Wearable Technology on Healthcare*
  https://www.otandp.com/blog/impact-of-wearable-technology-on-healthcare

- *Disrupting the Finance World: How Fintech is Changing the* ... https://execed.business.columbia.edu/disrupting-the-finance-world-how-fintech-is-changing-the-game-for-businesses

- *Augmented Reality in Education: Use Cases and Benefits*
  https://www.fingent.com/blog/augmented-reality-in-education-training-use-cases-and-business-benefits/

- *How AI in Retail is Revolutionizing the Shopping* ...
  https://appinventiv.com/blog/impact-of-ai-in-retail/

- *6 Examples of Industrial Robots in the Automotive Industry*
  https://www.universal-robots.com/blog/6-examples-of-industrial-robots-in-the-automotive-industry/

- *Blockchain in Supply Chain for Ecosystem Success*
  https://www.gartner.com/en/supply-chain/trends/blockchain-in-supply-chain

- *32 Big Data Examples & Applications*
  https://builtin.com/articles/big-data-examples-applications

- *Global views of social media and its impacts on society*
  https://www.pewresearch.org/global/2022/12/06/views-of-social-media-and-its-impacts-on-society-in-advanced-economies-2022/

- *Bias and Ethical Concerns in Machine Learning*
  https://www.isaca.org/resources/isaca-journal/issues/2022/volume-4/bias-and-ethical-concerns-in-machine-learning

- *Digital inclusion: Projects empowering global inclusion*
  https://www.weforum.org/agenda/2023/09/bridging-digital-divide-technology-empowering-global-inclusion/

- *The Evolution of the Internet, Identity, Privacy, and Tracking*
  https://iabtechlab.com/evolution-of-internet-identity-privacy-tracking/

- *Expert Methodologies for Technology Trend Analysis and ...*
  https://vollcomdigital.medium.com/expert-methodologies-for-technology-trend-analysis-and-forecasting-a4c44af1b2e6

- *The Power of AI: Market Trend Forecasting - Graphite Note*
  https://graphite-note.com/the-power-of-ai-market-trend-forecasting/#:~:text=AI%2Ddriven%20market%20trend%20forecasting,reducing%20the%20margin%20of%20error.

- *Government-led innovation acceleration: Case studies of ...* https://onlinelibrary.wiley.com/doi/full/10.1111/ropr.12474

- *These 7 tech trends will have the biggest impact on jobs* https://www.weforum.org/agenda/2023/05/workplace-technology-jobs-impact/

- *17 Types of Biohacking Technology to Transform Your Health* https://www.betterwayhealth.com/biohacking-technology

- *A look back on the BRAIN Initiative in 2023 (and what's coming in 2024)* https://braininitiative.nih.gov/news-events/blog/brain-initiative-alliance-look-back-brain-initiative-2023-and-whats-coming-2024#:~:text=BRAIN%20Initiative%20investigators%20made%20significant,with%20chronic%20pain%2C%20deep%20brain

- *Ethical and Scientific Issues of Nanotechnology in the ...* https://www.ncbi.nlm.nih.gov/pmc/articles/PMC1817662/

- *Mining in Space Is Coming* https://www.milkenreview.org/articles/mining-in-space-is-coming

- *The Trend of CRISPR-Based Technologies in COVID-19 ...* https://www.ncbi.nlm.nih.gov/pmc/articles/PMC8799426/

- *Geoengineering Solutions to Climate Change and Global ...* https://geoengineering.global/

- *Smart Water Management with IoT: Key Application Areas* https://www.softeq.com/blog/smart-water-management-using-iot-real-world-examples#:~:text=Smart%20Water%20Management%20for%20Agriculture,-With%20a%20growing&text=IoT%2Dbased%20systems%

20help%20farmers,accurately%20calculate%20crop%20wa
ter%20needs.

- *How blockchain technology can update global trade*
  https://www.cgai.ca/unblocking_the_bottlenecks_and_maki
  ng_the_global_supply_chain_transparent_how_blockchain
  _technology_can_update_global_trade